YOU HAVE SEVEN MESSAGES

YOU HAVE SEVEN MESSAGES

STEWART LEWIS

DELACORTE PRESS

WAIT IT OUT by IMOGEN JENNIFER JANE HEAP
© 2009 MEGAPHONIC LIMITED (NS)
All Rights Administered by WARNER/CHAPPELL MUSIC PUBLISHING LTD.
All Rights Reserved.
Used by Permission of ALFRED MUSIC PUBLISHING CO., INC.

Visit us on the Web! www.randomhouse.com/teens

Educators and librarians, for a variety of teaching tools, visit us at
www.randomhouse.com/teachers

Library of Congress Cataloging-in-Publication Data
Lewis, Stewart.
You have seven messages / Stewart Lewis. — 1st ed.
p. cm.
Summary: Teenaged Luna, who lives on Manhattan's Upper West Side with her movie director father, tries to piece together the death of her mother with the seven unheard messages left on her forgotten cell phone.
ISBN 978-0-385-74028-9 (trade) — ISBN 978-0-385-90832-0 (lib. bdg.) —
ISBN 978-0-375-89904-1 (ebook)
[1. Mothers—Fiction. 2. Death—Fiction. 3. New York (N.Y.)—Fiction.
4. Mystery and detective stories.] I. Title.
PZ7.L5881Yo 2011
[Fic]—dc22
2010032345

The text of this book is set in 11.5-point Berling.

Book design by Trish Parcell

Printed in the United States of America
10 9 8 7 6 5 4 3 2 1

First Edition

FOR MY MOM

ACKNOWLEDGMENTS

I'd like to thank first Emma Specter, who was the spark that ignited Luna, a character I feel I have somehow always known, and her musical muse, Imogen Heap, for her poetry and lush soundscapes.

Amelia Greene for her keen eye. Jessica Potts Lahey and Amy Chamberlin for being early, passionate readers. Jasmine Goguen for letting me pick her brain.

My dear friends and family who inspire and encourage me . . . the Foehls, Katrina Van Pelt, Hilary Old, Bill Candiloros, Flavia Stanley, Mia and Jeff, Paul Bosko, Susan Holland, Jennifer Phelps Montgomery, Ryan Daniel, Russell Swanson, Martin Hyatt, Vicka Tinetti, Bradford Noble, Michael Aisner, Leslie Novak, Nick Difruscia, Linda Yellen, Manuela Noble.

Stephen McCauley, Christopher Schelling, and Rebecca Barry for their unparalleled guidance and wit.

My skillful editor, Stephanie Elliott, for her hard work.

My agent, Mitchell Waters, for believing.

My daughter, Rowan, for her big open heart.

And lastly, Steve Swenson, my copilot.

I want to be with those
who know secret things
or else alone.
—*Rainer Maria Rilke*

Your absence has gone through me
Like thread through a needle.
Everything I do is stitched with its color.
—*W. S. Merwin*

CHAPTER 1

A LITTLE ABOUT MOI

I may be fourteen, but I read the *New York Times*. I don't wear hair clips or paint my cell phone with nail polish, and I'm not boy crazy. I don't have a subscription to *Twist* or *Bop* or *Flop* or whatever they call those glossy magazines full of posters of shiny-haired, full-lipped hunks.

Whatever you do, don't call me a tween. That makes me feel like I'm trapped in some adolescent purgatory where I get force-fed Disney-themed cupcakes while watching *Hannah Montana* reruns—that stage is over. Who came up with that name, anyway? I bet the person who came up with the name Hannah Montana gets paid a quarter of a million dollars a year and drives a Lexus. My cousin could've come up with a better name, and she's five and rides a tricycle.

I grew up in Manhattan on the Upper West Side, and

when I was really little, I thought my driver was my father. He'd take me to school every day and make sure my shoelaces were tied. Sometimes he'd let me listen to NPR while he chatted with the doormen. He seemed to know them all, a secret society of men in pressed black coats standing as straight as the buildings they protected. But of course, he wasn't my father. My *real* father is a film director who was at the height of his career when I was born, which is why he was never around. He was always shooting in places like Africa, Japan, Australia, and Canada. Now some critics say he's washed up, but I think the reason people become film critics is because they failed to be film directors themselves. I don't usually feel famous myself, but I went to the premiere of his last film (the one that supposedly washed him up) and a couple months later there was a picture of us in *Vanity Fair*. My over-enthusiastic English teacher, Ms. Gray, cut out the picture and taped it to the whiteboard. At first I was thrilled, but then I felt weird about it. I ended up sneaking in after class and bending the page so that you could only see my father, with his shiny face, his jet-black hair, and those wire-thin glasses that always seem to be sliding off his nose. He's the one who should be recognized. He literally spends *years* putting actors, writers, cinematographers, editors, studios, and locations all in a big blender until his movies pour out smoothly onto the screen. All I did that evening was walk next to him and carry the cheat sheet for his speech.

My little brother, Tile, was too young to come to the

premiere with us or have his photo taken. When my mom was pregnant with him, the only thing that helped her nausea was lying on the cold Spanish tile in our townhouse bathroom, so that became his name. Everyone calls him Kyle by mistake.

My uncle, a professor who lives in Italy, gave me a small book of Shakespeare's sonnets for my tenth birthday, and sometimes I read Tile my favorite ones. Even though he's ten, he pretends to understand them. I think he just likes the musical way the words go together. Tile is a good listener, and he leaves me alone pretty much every time I ask him to. If a genie said I could wish for any little brother in the whole world, I would stick with Tile. He smells nice and never talks with his mouth full. He also keeps my secrets.

Here's one: I know I told you that I'm not boy crazy, mostly because boys are dirty and unpredictable, but there is one I've had my eye on since I was eight. He is very clean. He lives across the street and our drivers are friends. He goes to a school somewhere outside the city. I like to imagine it's an exotic place like Barbados, but it's probably in Westchester. He's only said ten words to me in seven years. Sometimes when I read Shakespeare's sonnets I think of his big mop of strawberry curls, and the way he swings his book bag in wide circles.

So are you to my thoughts as food to life,
Or as sweet-season'd showers are to the ground

He's one year older than me, and his name is Oliver. He walks with a peculiar grace, almost like he's floating. He also plays the cello, and he's so good at it that when I listen to him through my bedroom window, the tiny hairs on my arms stick up.

Sometimes I lie on my bed imagining the music was written just for me, coming in through the window as a personal serenade. Music sounds better when you close your eyes.

CHAPTER 2

THEN THERE WERE THREE

Tile and I are on spring break, so on our driver's day off, we take the subway to the zoo in the Bronx. I love to look at all the different kinds of people on the train and try to eavesdrop on their thoughts for just a minute. I notice Tile's feet hanging off the seat, not able to touch the ground. My feet have touched the ground since I was six. People think it's great to be tall, but it's not when you're a young girl. Once when I tried talking to some boys at our school dance I had to crouch down like I was their Little League coach.

The train makes a loud screeching noise and Tile inches closer to my dad. This might be the first time we are actually going on an outing as a family of three. I uncurl my fingers and look down at my hands. They are my mother's, thin and delicate. I think of the last line from the poem that is stenciled onto the wall in my father's office: *nobody, not even the rain, has such small hands.* Maybe what the author meant is that every person is completely unique. Every raindrop, every pair of hands, everyone on this train.

When my father came to my camp in New Hampshire almost a year ago in the middle of the summer, I knew something was terribly wrong. I was sailing on the lake, but suddenly I saw him on the dock, looking out over the water and wearing his light blue Windbreaker. He was supposed to have been in Scotland shooting a movie. When I saw the camp director next to him, waving frantically to my counselor to sail back, I *really* knew something wasn't right. When we reached the dock and I jumped from the boat, my father kneeled down and hugged me so tight I could barely breathe. He cried into my hair.

Your mother is gone and she's never coming back.

The words caught in his throat, and it was a voice I had never heard come out of him. I instantly knew he meant *gone,* as in forever. That she hadn't simply run away or skipped town.

"What?"

"It was an accident. In the city. She got hit. . . ."

I wanted to slap him across the face. How could he tell me this? How could my mother, so vibrant and alive, just suddenly be *gone?* Accidents happened in Manhattan every day—but not to my mother. Everything suddenly felt terribly unfair. I looked up at the trees surrounding the lake, the wispy clouds slowly becoming drained of color.

"Do you think she's in the sky or in the ground?" I asked him.

I thought he said "Both," but it might have been "Oh."

I couldn't cry. I remember looking at my own reflection in the water, thinking of Narcissus, who died falling in love with his own reflection. I could've died right there, because the thought of living without someone you love is like a pair of giant hands pressing around your heart, making it smaller and smaller, until you are left with only a memory of warmth. It's like when the sun comes through a window, moving across the room with each hour, until night falls and all you can do is try to remember the soothing shapes it made.

CHAPTER 3

TRUTH

The whole way back from the zoo I feel like people are whispering about my dad. I want to tell them to mind their own business. When tragedy happens to people who are famous, it is treated more like a scandal—what people don't realize is yes, my dad made some pretty iconic movies, but deep down he is vulnerable just like everyone else.

My mother once told me that the truth is like my skin, a beautiful, protective covering, and the things people say or think are like clothes that can be easily changed or discarded. She told me truth comes from your heart.

When I was ten, there was a rumor spread about my father and an underage actress he had never even met. School turned into pure hell, and everyone shunned me. It was amazing how much venom people had, like a tabloid was even trustworthy.

One morning my mother marched into my PE class and didn't even bother telling the teacher she was taking me. She just gave her the Look, as she did into so many cameras all over the world: *Don't mess with me.* She didn't tell me where we were going until we got there, two hours later. It was her friend's old house on the Hudson River, with screened-in porches that had antique beds on them. He was a chef, and he made us macaroni and cheese with shaved truffles. She'd pulled strings with the AV guy at my school, who she knew from a shoot long before, and got him to hunt down and fax all my homework assignments. It was her way of helping me deal with the rumor thing: home school for a week. I loved it, even though I missed Tile. He was so cute at that time, a little nugget.

On our last night there was tons of moonlight and we had ice cream on the porch. It was the kind of moment where you remember every detail. Mint chocolate chip. Three boats, one called *Seas the Day.* It was there, in front of the glassy river so bright it could have been a mirror, that my mother told me about truth.

"But how do you really know what's true? Is there some big book of truth?"

She laughed. When my mother laughed she looked like an angel, that's what my father always said. Her big eyes looked up, squinting a little, and she would slightly shake her head, like a happy dog.

"The book is in here." She placed her hand where my heart is.

"Yes, but why do people just make things up?" [1]

"Usually because they are bored, or insecure. There was this gossip website that used to print all this stuff about me. At first I was really angry, you know, like you probably were with those kids. Then, I remember going to an opening gala, I think it was for a fragrance of some kind . . . anyway, there were all these celebrities there, and none of them looked at me strange or had even bought into the rumors. And I realized that all of them had lies written about them all the time, but they were above it, you know? They were secure in who they were."

"What do you mean?"

She turned toward me and ran her fingers down the side of my face.

"Do you remember the time you wanted to wear that green hat, the one that was too big for you, that you found on one of your father's sets?"

"Yes."

"We tried to get you to rethink wearing it to school, but when we dropped you off, you owned it. You walked with confidence. That is being secure."

"Well, more like stupid."

She laughed again, and the angel came through her. Then she put on her serious face and said, "No choice is stupid if it comes from you. And you, you are . . . you are the most beautiful girl in the whole world, inside and out. Never let anyone take away the choices in your heart; it's what makes you one of a kind."

She had lost me a little, but I got the idea.

"I mean, if you want to look like Kermit the Frog, go for it!"

This time I laughed. Then I heard a car crunching down the gravel driveway. It was our driver. I remember running up with Mom because I thought it might be Tile, but it was my father coming up from the city to surprise us. He had stolen away from his film set to visit for the night. He had a large bouquet of flowers for Mom and a huge lollipop for me. I grabbed the lollipop and went to the hammock.

The stars were like a million fireflies, and I remember feeling so safe, like nothing could ever touch me. I looked inside and all the lights were on. My father was coaxing my mother out of the kitchen chair, and they started to dance. My father looked like a boy, and he had so much hope, so much wonder in his eyes, that I secretly wished someone like him would love me someday.

CHAPTER 4

THE NEXT STEP

The zoo is crowded today, and the animals look really bored. But no matter how many people stare at them, they don't act vain. Kind of like my mother. She was a model, but not really because she liked to be looked at. It was a way for her to make a lot of money in a little time, so she could do what she really wanted to do—write. Her book was optioned by my father, which was how they met. My father claimed she wanted nothing to do with him at first. Even after the movie was made, she barely took his calls. It wasn't until they ran into each other years later at a party for *Paper* magazine that my dad spotted her across the room, and decided then and there he would stop at nothing to win her over. He sent her flowers every day for a month.

Seeing my father now, spilling his sno-cone while the

depressed lions pace around, I feel a sharp sadness for him. Things weren't supposed to turn out this way. As Tile runs his fingers through the water fountain that doesn't turn off, I brush the tiny pieces of crushed blue ice off Dad's button-down shirt.

After getting home from camp—that horrible day on the dock—my father and I didn't really know how to grieve. We didn't talk much, but we took comfort in each other, and we still do, now more than ever.

"It's been almost a year since Mom died, you know."

"Really?" he says, pushing up his glasses.

"Don't you think you should maybe try and date someone?" Saying the words makes me feel horrible, like I'm betraying my own mother. But somehow I know I'm right, and maybe it's what she would've wanted.

"Funny you should mention that." He holds up a finger and touches my cheek with it. "I have a date on Tuesday."

"You do?" Now I wish I hadn't said anything. Now I want to build a brick wall around my father's heart.

"Not even sure what I'm going to do."

"Be yourself," I offer. "What's her name?"

He tilts the sno-cone up to swallow the last bit, then crumples the paper in his hand. As we walk toward the monkeys, he starts to laugh. "I don't remember . . . something with an *E* . . . Ella?"

I realize it's the first time I've heard my father laugh in a year. I desperately want him to forget someone else's name.

"Well, you should maybe figure that out before the date."

His broad smile gives me hope. Maybe the E-word will be funny and kind and strong like my mother was. Or maybe she'll just want to be in one of his movies, which would be even sadder than seeing drugged-up lions in a cage.

The bird sanctuary is unimpressive. Underneath the white canopy, they can barely fly. I prefer birds in real life. Once when I was at camp I saw four loons flying across the lake together, and they were so smooth and effortless. The sunset looked like a giant wound in the sky and I could see their reflections, silhouettes on the water's surface. All at once they landed with a flourish, as if choreographed, perfectly calculated.

My father buys Tile a big paper eagle at the gift store and we leave the zoo and go to a café where the waitresses all have weaves in their hair. The hostess pats my head as she sits us down. My dad orders a beer and I notice something in his eyes, some sort of light that wasn't there. After the accident his eyes turned gray and cloudy, and now they are blue and clear again. I take a big breath and stretch my legs onto the empty seat. This is the problem, though. Right when I start to feel like everything's going to be all right, I'm reminded in some way that my mother isn't here, sitting in this empty seat that my feet rest on. We're not a complete unit, like the loons.

"Moon, don't put your feet up on that."

My father calls me Moon because it was my first word. Apparently they would take me onto the roof when I was a baby to see the moon every night before bed, and if it wasn't there I'd cry myself to sleep.

I take my feet down and wipe the chair with my napkin. As we eat our meal I keep turning to the empty seat, expecting to see Mom's long eyelashes, her curvy nose, her fragile hands.

On the subway home, I think about writing a letter to Oliver. If I could write something as beautiful as the music he plays, maybe we'd be destined to be together. Even though I know from experience that life is not a romantic comedy, something about his curly hair, his fluid walk, and his cello playing makes me feel like the girl walking down the street during the opening credits.

CHAPTER 5

PIED-À-TERRE

On Thursday, garbage day, the trucks sound like distant monsters screaming their terrible sounds. I wake up at the first high-pitched squeal, roll out of bed, and shuffle into the bathroom. There's no pen or pad, so I write on toilet paper with an eyeliner pencil:

> *There once was a boy with impossible curls*
> *Watched from afar by a curious girl*
> *Listening through the open window*
> *She pictured his hands gripping the bow*
> *Making the deepest sound she ever heard*
> *Nothing that could ever be described by a word*

The bathroom door opens, and Tile walks in rubbing his eyes, his hair in disarray. He takes the poem out of my hand and reads it, then makes a noise that hints of approval. He's my perfect audience. I grab it back and leave so he can pee in private.

Today's the day I've decided to go to my mother's studio, which has basically been untouched since she died. I feel like there may be something there that will bring me closer to her. On the way to school I have our driver go past it, to get a picture of it in my mind, so I can mentally prepare throughout the day. It's on the top floor of a skinny brownstone near the park. Since two of the walls are glass, it resembles an urban greenhouse. It's small but has a lot of *charm*, as real estate people say. My father went there once a few weeks after she died, but he couldn't bring himself to move anything. To this day, the place remains as my mother left it, and none of us has gone in there.

It's "green" week at school, so everyone is acting like they care about our environment. After the week is over most people will go back to using Styrofoam cups, driving massive SUVs to the Hamptons, and letting the water run while they brush their teeth. But it's nice to raise awareness, and I'm trying to be a half-full instead of a half-empty girl.

My dad's not there when I get home from school, so I go into his office and search the key drawer. At the bottom is a large key with a piece of masking tape stuck to it, the word *studio* written with a red Sharpie. My heart pinches at the sight of my mother's wavy handwriting. I stare at the key in my open hand for a minute and then curl my fingers around it.

My neighbor smiles at me when I walk by. I'm allowed to go out alone as long as it's light out. It takes me fifteen minutes, and when I get to the front of the brownstone I realize I'm sweating. I take a deep breath and start to climb the steps.

I don't take the elevator because it's the size of a phone booth. On the landing of the fourth floor, I pass a cleaning lady who's listening to one of those old Walkmans that play cassettes. . . . Does anyone have those anymore? She grins and puts her hand on my shoulder. Even though she seems supernice, I cannot wait for the day when people stop petting me like I'm an animal.

I get to the door, which says 6b but the *b* is broken and hangs down to look like a *q*. I slowly turn the key and push the door open.

The first thing I see is what might have been an apple in a big silver bowl. Now it looks more like a prune with a green blanket of mold wrapped around it, half eaten by bugs. I open the window and then dump the decomposed apple in the garbage, then go to the fridge. I am relieved to find there's nothing in it except some condiments and a bottle of white wine. I go back down to the cleaning lady and ask her if I can borrow some rags and her Windex. She doesn't understand English, but I show her what I need, like a charade, and she smiles and hands me the bottle, a rag, and a feather duster. I spend the next hour cleaning the half inch of dust covering everything. I open Mom's laptop and am taken aback by the screen saver. It's a picture of me on the beach in Nantucket. I'm not smiling. I look cold and annoyed, but my gaze is sharp.

A large tear goes *splat* on the keyboard.

The bedroom alcove is the size of a closet but has lots of light. I try to smell her in the crumpled sheets, but they're old and musty. I peel them off quickly and pile them in the corner. I see a black cord peeking from her desk drawer. I pull it out and take in a shallow breath. It's her cell phone, the charger still attached. I plug it in to see if it still works, amazed at the sound of it booting up. I guess my father didn't even bother canceling her service. Maybe it was a family plan and he wanted to keep it that way. She wasn't one of those people who always had her cell phone on her—it took her forever to even get one. I go down her list of contacts and stop at Marc Jacobs. When I was nine, I actually had tea in Paris with him. My mother was a fashion model, and one day when she went on a "go-see" for French *Vogue* she left me with Marc at a café in the Marais. His fingers were long and tanned, and he had kind eyes. At the time I thought he was just some guy. Now I think about that afternoon every time I wear my favorite low-cut blue dress, from his 2001 spring collection, made especially for my mother but passed on to me. I press Call. It goes straight to his voice mail and I don't leave a message. I am too stunned that I am in my mother's studio, calling Marc Jacobs, a trail of big tears drying on my face.

I decide to take a shower in the tiny black-and-white-tiled bathroom. I watch the dust from the tub swirl down the drain and think, *That's what she is now.* I dry off and get dressed again, collapsing on the naked mattress. I briefly think of what it would be like to bring Oliver here. Maybe he could play the cello while I made him baked salmon. A few days after my mother died I found a recipe in the newspaper for baked salmon, and I made it for my father, along with asparagus, his favorite vegetable. When he came home and saw me with the apron that went all the way to the floor, my face sweaty from the steam, he started to cry. Seeing a grown man cry is heartbreaking but also beautiful. We hardly put a dent in the salmon, but what we ate tasted good.

I turn my head and see something that makes my throat tighten: a cuff link on the nightstand, made to look like a sad theater mask. *What is it doing here?* I pick it up and blow the dust off it. As far as I know, the only cuff links my dad has are the ones that look like little rope knots. Besides, this is not the sort of thing he would wear. I look underneath the bed for the happy face, but there's nothing there except more dust and a stray button.

Hmmmm. I run the cuff link through my fingers, like it's a key to some language I'm not sure I want to learn. My mother never mentioned entertaining guests at her studio—it was her own private space. But somebody was here. Somebody who was not my father.

I remember one day in eighth grade I skipped soccer practice and came home early and went up to my mother's room. We had a ritual where we'd sit on the bed and I'd tell her everything that happened that day. Even when the details of the day were boring, she would find ways to make them exciting. Like when I told her I had a math test and ate chicken tenders for lunch she explained that math was a way to get your mind to think a certain way, and even though it seems tedious, it's the basis for everything in the world. Then she'd tell me that chickens lose their feathers when they get stressed. Basically, my mother could weave a colorful conversation out of a pile of dirt. That day I actually had something kind of exciting to tell her—we had a bomb threat, and my science teacher brought his dog in for an experiment, and it got so excited that it peed on his desk, which was hilarious—but she was in the bath, not expecting me so early. She was talking to someone on the phone in a honeyed tone that made me feel like I shouldn't be eavesdropping. Still, I listened. It was almost like she was singing.

As I turn the cuff link over in my hand, the memory lodges itself in the bottom of my stomach like an undercooked pancake. Could the person she was talking to that day be the owner? I had an inkling there was more to learn about her death, but this was not what I had in mind.

Back in the living room, the air is starting to freshen up since I opened the small window in the bathroom for cross-ventilation. I go back to the computer and look at the folders on her desktop. One says "Stuff" and one says "Modeling." In the bottom corner, another says "Luna," her version of my nickname, and basically what everyone calls me. In fact, the only person who calls me Malia, my real name, is the school nurse. I look at the folder again, and I cannot bring myself to double-click on it. It's probably just pictures and stuff, but there are so many emotions coursing through me that I can almost feel my brain uncurling like a flower blooming on fast-forward video. I look outside and notice it's almost dark. I shut down the laptop, close the window, grab the trash along with the duster and the Windex, and head down the stairs. The woman is still there. I place the stuff neatly on the floor and say *"Gracias,"* and she smiles. One of the things I learned from my father is if you use words from other people's languages it makes them smile. Whenever we go to my favorite Thai place near Times Square, I always say *"kop khun kha"* to the waitress when she serves our food, and she gives me an extra Coke on the house.

On the way home I stop and buy peanuts. Chewing them helps distract me from the questions that flutter around my mind like frantic insects. *Who is the owner of the cuff link? What's in my folder?*

As I reach Central Park West, I am startled by a buzz in my pocket. Mom's phone! I open it up and the screen reads, *7 new messages.* As if it's a bomb that might go off, I quickly turn it off and head into our building.

I go upstairs and lock the door to my room. I look at the phone again and think, *This is a dead person's phone.*

My mother was very open with me, but her personal life was just that: personal. Would she want me to have this? Who are the messages from? I squeeze the stress ball Dad gave me and think about this past year, how much I have been through, how much I have lost. In order to preserve my sanity, I cannot listen to the messages right away, and if I do, maybe only one at a time. Maybe I'm just being dramatic, but something about finding the cuff link has made me question what was really going on in my mother's life.

I try to focus on my homework but before long I hear Oliver practicing. I go over to the window and stare across the street. The angle only allows me to see a corner of his cello, and the tip of the bow if he holds a long note. I put my mother's phone under the mattress and lie down.

When adults use the word *overwhelmed*, I always think it's just an excuse to get attention, but now I understand what it means. I decide to close my eyes and just listen to Oliver. I take deep breaths and try to let the music seep through my skin, into my bones. It's a trick my drama teacher told us about, for relaxation. It works for a while, but then all I can picture is the little red phone, shoved under the mattress, and I imagine it pulsing like a heartbeat.

CHAPTER 6

I DARE YOU

I don't tell anyone I've been to the studio. It's my secret. Today is crystal clear and everyone in New York seems to carry the promise of spring in their waving hands, their scooping arms, and their buoyant steps. I walk deep into the park and find a bench in the shade. I get out Mom's phone and dial her voice mail. It asks for a password. *Damn.*

I'm clutching the phone so hard my knuckles are white. I try her birth date. No luck. Then I try our address. Nope. I sit back and look up at the expanse of blue sky with one small lonely cloud. I think of my dad, who would say, "Look, a storm's coming in." And then it appears in my vision. A little obscured by a giant tree, looking like a withered white balloon.

I type in *luna* and the voice says, *"You have seven messages. To listen to your messages, press one."*

My fingers are shaking. I tell myself, *One at a time.* That way it won't all come crashing down on me. I do what the voice tells me.

Beep.

I can hardly understand the thick Asian accent, but at the end she says the word *pickup*, so I figure it's Mom's dry-cleaning place. I hit 7 for Delete and head to Seventy-Sixth Street. Or is it Seventy-Seventh? I remember they had terrible candies in a bowl. One day my mother got mad at me for spitting one out on someone's stoop. She said it wasn't ladylike.

I recognize the small blue awning and go inside. Sure enough, the candies are still there. There's a Chinese girl, maybe sixteen, who gives me a challenging look. I'm not exactly sure why I've come here. Surely they don't still have her clothes?

I stutter a few times until the mother comes in and recognizes me, gives me that look of pity I'm so tired of. She must have heard about my mother's death from the neighborhood women gossiping. Or maybe she reads Page Six, which is doubtful. She has a bob haircut and wears a brown cardigan. Her fingers are dry and twisted. She holds them up as if telling me to wait. The daughter keeps looking at me, except now with a blank expression. The bell that's tied to the door rattles and a woman comes in, dressed in a tight black skirt and silver heels. It takes me a second to realize it's Oliver's mom. My heartbeat quickens as I see a shadow behind the door, a boy following her in.

I start to take inventory of what I have on. Jeans and a red shirt that's faded to orange. Oh no, the wrong shoes—they make my feet look too big. I peek over at Oliver, who is swinging his book bag and definitely not noticing my shoes. I see him reach out for a candy and I blurt out a sound to make him stop.

"You really don't want to eat those," I whisper.

He looks at me, really, for the first time, and smiles. I feel like my skin is on fire and any moment I will self-combust. His eyelashes are overgrown and his lips are violet. The fluorescent light makes a thin halo around his curls.

In what seems like an hour, the lady comes back with my mother's dress. She hands it to me along with a bill. Is she going to charge me? I look over at Oliver, who looks at the floor. The lady nods and waves her gnarled fingers again and I turn to leave, but not before giving Oliver my best smile.

I don't think my mother even owned a pair of shorts—she always wore dresses. When I was little, I would constantly hide under them. The skirt part would become my own personal tent with her smooth, tanned legs as the poles.

When I get home I immediately rip open the plastic, which is lined with paper advertising the cleaners. It's a black dress, with tiny gold beading along the collar and on the hem. I can't remember my mother ever wearing it. I try it on and look in the mirror. It's the most beautiful thing I've ever worn. I turn around and go to the window. I can sense someone has been watching me. There's no one there but the light is on. After a few seconds the light goes off and a figure approaches the window. All I can see is the silhouette of curly hair. I smile and turn around, showing off the dress, and then pull the curtain.

I want to show my father but I don't want to jog his memory in a bad way. I tiptoe past Tile's room and see him sleeping on the floor next to his bed. It's hard to maneuver in the dress but I manage to get him back up and under the covers. Half asleep, he says, "Mom?"

I take a step back and watch him. His nostrils flare a little as if he smells something in a dream. He purses his lips and turns over. I creep down the stairs and stop on the last step, stunned by a female voice I don't recognize laughing nervously. The E-word!

Before I can turn around and run back up the stairs, they enter the foyer on their way out. The E-word is pretty in a raw, bohemian way. My father stops short at the sight of the dress. I cannot see myself, but I know my face is the color of tomato soup. I realize he's never seen my mother wearing it.

"Moon," my father says, "where . . . what . . . ?"

"I went by the dry cleaner, you know, the one . . ."

Luckily, the E-word breaks the awkward silence and holds out her hand. She has on leather jewelry. "I'm Elise, so nice to meet you."

"You as well."

"Going somewhere?" she asks, almost taunting me.

"Yes," I say, "I'm just gonna go crawl under a rock. You have a nice night, both of you." I try to give my father a go-for-it look as they smile and walk past. I notice a tag hanging down the back of his jacket and it takes me two tugs to rip it off. When I get back to my room I peer out the window down to the street. They are standing very close, waiting for a cab. I go to my bed and sit down.

She smelled nice, what was it . . . apricot?

I take off the dress and put on my nightshirt. It's really hard to concentrate on homework, but I try. All I keep thinking about is Oliver, the way he finally *saw* me at the dry cleaner. Does he know I've been watching him or that I listen to him practice? Then I think about my mother's phone, six more messages. I decide to wait until tomorrow. The scene on the stairs was traumatic enough.

As I get into bed, I wonder what Dad and Elise are doing on their date. Elise reminds me of my camp counselor, Willow, who always looked glassy-eyed and wore a half smile. She was the total opposite of my mom, whose eyes were always alert, almost startled, and whose mouth was always slightly pursed. I have that mouth too. It's kind of a pain because people sometimes think I'm frowning when I'm just thinking. I look up at the picture of my mother, still stuck to my wall with an inch of Scotch tape. It came from one of those huge glossy magazines they put in hotels. She's wearing a shiny dress with a furry collar and her look says *I dare you.*

CHAPTER 7

MOON OVER BROOKLYN

It's spring break, and my father has finally finished his documentary, so while Tile watches cartoons, we eat the one thing Dad likes to make—french toast.

"Why did you go to the dry cleaner?" he says, lips shiny with syrup.

I try to fill my mouth with food quickly so I can think of a response.

"Just curious, I guess."

He stops chewing and gives me a look I cannot decipher, then takes another bite.

"How was your date?" I say, changing the subject.

"It was . . . fine," he replies.

My father has always been hard to read. He gives you what he wants to give and nothing more.

"Is she a pot dealer?"

He laughs. The simple sound of it warms me up.

"She's a teacher," he says.

"Let me guess, basket weaving?"

He laughs again, but this time it's a chuckle. The pot dealer line clearly had more punch.

"She teaches English. She's nice enough. It's just . . ."

He doesn't have to finish the sentence. We both know what he means. It's hard enough for *me* to imagine someone taking Mom's place, but no doubt harder for *him*. I cut out the center of my french toast, the best bit.

"You know Oliver, from across the street?"

"I've seen him around."

"Hypothetically, if he invited me, do you think I could go listen to him practice the cello?"

He forks in another bite and wipes at each corner of his mouth. "I suppose that would be fine."

"I'm going to be fifteen in three days."

"I know, Moon. I'm not *that* out of it."

I can tell by his expression that I have room to tease. "No, but for a while there you just wandered around from room to room. I almost called Bellevue."

He throws his napkin at me but I dodge it just in time.

The truth is, after the accident, I walked around like that too. Tile went to live with my grandmother on Long Island for three months and Dad and I became zombies, living on Thai food and ginger ale. I went through the motions at school, dropping from an A to a C average, and lost my friends, the two Rachels. I'm not even sure why we had remained friends before; it just sort of happened. In fifth grade we won an art project we did together on Valentine's Day. While all the other kids did these simple cutout hearts with construction paper, we took pictures of all kinds of couples at our parents' dinner parties or in the park. Gay and straight, white and black, young and old, smiling and goofing around. We arranged them in a giant heart and the teacher displayed it for the whole year. The Rachels and I were constantly doing creative things together, and hiding out while our parents had cocktails. Now, Rachel One is a pretty-on-the-outside shell of a girl who spends four hundred dollars a month on her hair and is dating half of Central Park West. Rachel Two is basically mute—she rarely talks and is more like a pretty bag Rachel One carries around. I call them Barbots—part Barbie, part robot. They starve themselves, are addicted to lip gloss, and wear their insecurity on their Prada sleeves. After my mother died, they couldn't understand why I wasn't grieving outwardly, why I didn't seem sad. Rachel One said my behavior was "creepy," and Rachel Two (in a rare use of words) said that I just didn't "fit in" anymore. I didn't really blame them. Some inner mechanism in me shut down and I couldn't feel anything. They defriended me on Facebook and I didn't really care.

Now I mostly hang out with Janine "Oscar" Myers—probably 'cause we're both outsiders. Her claim to fame is far more controversial than mine—she made a video for her boyfriend of herself eating a hot dog with suspicious gusto, only to have him plaster it all over the Internet. I actually thought it was funny, but the Gossip Girls at our school (seniors who dress like they're on the show) held her down in the bathroom and wrote SLUT on her forehead. I tried to help her wash it off but there wasn't time. She ended up going through the rest of classes with it still faintly there. The Rachels wouldn't even look at me after I befriended her, but it was just as well. After I lost Mom, their obsession with things like lip gloss and that android Zac Efron seemed completely unimportant.

I pick up our sticky dishes and bring them to the sink. As I turn on the water my dad says, "I'll do it, Moonlight."

When he uses that particular variation of my nickname, I can feel his love so strongly it's almost palpable. There was a long period of time when that word, that tone of his voice, had gone missing, like a favorite pair of earrings you're not sure how you lost. You feel like they're in the house somewhere, ready to surprise you at any minute.

"Cool," I say, and run upstairs. I retrieve the red cell phone and put it in my back pocket. On my way out, my father calls from the sink, "Cello practice already?"

"I wish," I call back. "Just going for a walk."

"Okay, please be careful!"

"I'll find the nearest creepy guy with a van," I say. He winces as I close the door.

Everyone on the street is still infused with spring. You

can see it in their bright clothes, their hopeful faces. I find the nearest stoop that looks out-of-the-way and retrieve message number six. Seeing my father almost normal has given me a sense of calm, and my fingers are not shaking this time.

It's a man's deep voice with some sort of accent, Australian, maybe. He calls her "love" and tells her she must "pop over." He leaves an address in a place called Greenpoint, in Brooklyn.

If my mother's personal life was once off-limits to me, can it really be now? Why did the dress from the dry cleaner surprise Dad so much? Did it have to do with the owner of the cuff link? I walk through the park to the East Side and get into a cab.

"Forty-Four Eagle Street, Greenpoint."

The driver looks at me with suspicion.

"Don't worry, I've got plenty of money and I'm allowed to travel alone."

This seems to work. He throws up his hands and starts the meter.

I'm not sure what I'm really trying to find, but something beyond my control is taking over. I don't want to bother my father about it, especially since he's in good spirits, but I need to know more.

Going across the Pulaski Bridge, I can see most of downtown, the buildings strong and proud above the river. I am looking at a city of eight million people, none of them my mother.

Eagle Street looks industrial, with one lone deli on the corner. The building stretches the length of the whole block and looks like it was once a factory. There are several kids on skateboards carrying squirt guns. They must be on spring break too.

I have the cab wait for me and I enter the building. At the far end of the block some hipsters are doing a photo shoot, and there's trash swirling in the wind. The door has been propped open, so I wander into the stairway, which smells of wax and cigarette smoke. I climb the stairs, gaining adrenaline. Outside 3B, I stand there, mystified.

What am I looking for?

Before I knock, the door opens and a man with a goatee, in a sport coat, smiles at me as I jump back.

"Can I help you?"

It's the same accent. The deep voice. I stand there, until words somehow find their way out of my mouth. "Did you know Marion Clover?"

The man pauses, his mouth open a little, then looks at me suspiciously, like I may be dangerous.

"Yes, of course, why do you ask?"

"She was my mother."

His face melts a little, as if he might cry; then he sweeps his arm into the space and says, "Why don't you come in."

The place is vast and uncluttered. The old windows have dozens of little panes the size of paperbacks, and through them you can see the entire Manhattan skyline. He removes a cowboy hat from a big green chair and says, "Here, sit."

I sit down gently. I notice he is wearing an old T-shirt and jeans. He doesn't seem to be someone who regularly wears cuff links, but I can't be sure.

"Luna, right?"

For some reason hearing him say my mom's version of my nickname, and what has basically become my real name, makes me want to cry. I nod slowly and try to regain composure.

"I'm Benjamin."

"From Australia?"

"South Africa."

Wow, not even close. Looking into Benjamin's deep-set pale brown eyes, I realize I don't even know what to ask him. I start with the obvious.

"How did you know my mother?"

"Hang on a minute. Does your pop know you're here?"

"No. I have a cab waiting, though. I'm not supposed to leave Manhattan, but I can see it right there." I point to the windows. "Close enough, right?"

"How did you—"

"You left a message, on her cell phone. Why did you give this address?"

The door swings open and in walks a woman with legs that probably go up to my ears. She has on a thin, tight sweater and her lipstick is such a dark red it looks like blood. In fact, she is rolling the lipstick case through her hands. She looks at Benjamin for an explanation of my presence. He doesn't say anything, so she turns to me and says, "Daria."

"My neighbor," Benjamin adds.

"Well," I say, standing up, "I'm sorry to come over unannounced."

"It's okay," he says. "Your mother was my muse for a while. I'm a painter, and a graphic designer. Some of my best work is of her. I can show you. Anyway, she was always saying she wanted to see my new place, and one day she finally agreed to; that's why I left the message. I am so sorry about what happened."

Daria slinks onto the couch, staring at Benjamin. The phone rings and he picks it up immediately, like he's desperately awaiting the call.

He's gone for several minutes, during which Daria stares at me like she's reading a book. I try to be like my father and show blank pages.

"You lost your mom," she says with a thick accent. Swedish?

"Yes," I say.

"So did I. When I was a little younger than you."

She must be a model. She has overblown features and a languid way of being, like so many of them. "I'm sorry," I say, even though I usually hate it when people tell me that. Sorry doesn't bring people back.

"Did you ever think about getting, you know—" She's

pointing to my chest. In order to avoid hearing the words *training bra* out loud, I cut her off.

"Yes, I have one, I just don't have it on," I lie. I cannot bear telling her I'm way late on the whole bra thing. "Did you . . . did you know my mother?"

"No, but I read her book." She places the lipstick on the end table. "It was devastatingly accurate."

"Accurate about what?" I ask.

"The misperception of the general public toward models."

I think about this. Everyone can be misunderstood, whether you're a model or not. She could've come up with a better remark, but I let it slide.

"She didn't like models," I say, even though I'm not really sure. I think she just avoided telling people she was a model.

Daria looks at me intently.

"I bet she loved you."

I don't know what to say to this. Of course she did, but I don't want to brag about it. Then I remember my father saying one should always accept compliments with grace.

"She did." I smile, noticing a pen and a hotel pad on the table. "Listen, I'm going to leave my email address on this pad, 'cause I've got to get back to the city. Could you give it to Benjamin? I want to see the work he did with my mother sometime."

"Of course," she says, standing up. Her arms are gangly

like spider legs, and she smells like Chanel No. 5. I know because it was the only scent my mother wore. She pats me on the head, walks toward the bathroom, and says, "Nice to meet you, sweetie."

The head patting puts a damper on the adventure. Do I look like I'm five? I write my email and my IM name on the pad, and before I leave, I take the lipstick, open it, and put some on.

The cabbie is still there when I get back outside. Now that I have the lipstick on, he gives me an even stranger look.

On the way back into the city, I think of what I really knew about my mother. I knew her smell, and that she rarely cooked. I remember her big eyes, her angel laugh, her delicate hands. The way she could turn from being playful to completely serious, and how I rarely could get anything past her. I put on my seat belt and roll down the window, letting the air at my face. I close my eyes and remember that tonight is usually when Oliver plays, and a slight shudder travels through me.

CHAPTER 8

PLAN OF ATTACK

I make it back to the safety of my room and smile because I was right. He's doing scales. They aren't as pretty as what he usually plays, but I still love the sound. I know it's a little "Kumbaya" to say this, but it makes me feel more connected to everything.

A few times he stops abruptly, and I imagine he's listening for me, sensing me. I wish I could build a secret walkway across the street from our two windows.

When he's finished, I check my email and see one from Daria, the girl in Benjamin's apartment.

> Hi there—
> Benjamin ran off and I never got to give him your email.
> I tell you what, if you want, let's go shopping on Saturday.

Why don't you meet me at Strawberry Fields in
Central Park at two?
Ciao,
Daria

My dad peeks his head in without knocking, which annoys me. He's wearing his fuzzy gray robe. "Hey, Moonbeam, what's up?"

I quickly minimize the screen so he can't see the email. "Nothing. Just looking at Internet porn."

He smiles, but then his face gets all twisted up, and I realize I still have the lipstick on. I try to think of something quick.

"I was fooling around at Sephora."

He sits down on the floor and starts playing with a scarf I have hanging on the back of the door. "Elise is here," he says.

I am not prepared for this information.

"That was fast," I reply.

"Yes, it was. I'm not even sure what I'm doing, but I want to . . . I want to make sure you're okay with it."

What am I supposed to say to this? *Yes, it's fine, just tell the hippie lady to move in?*

"I'm okay with it as long as you are."

He stands up and paces around my room, the scarf wrapped around his hands.

"You know, every time I think I'm moving forward, that just maybe I can be a normal person in the world, I see you."

He stops and puts a hand to my face, draws an imaginary comma on my cheek. I turn away and wipe off the lipstick with a tissue.

"You have her eyes, her smile, her quick mind. You're everything that was great about her."

I try to stop tears from pushing out.

"Were there things that weren't great about her?"

He puts the scarf around me and says, "Well, there were certain sides of her life she never showed me. I think everyone has those sides." He puts the scarf back on the hook and turns to me. "Are there things you feel, thoughts you have, that are only for you, completely private?"

I think about Oliver and his cello, and my mother's phone under the mattress.

"Yes."

"Well, I think that Elise is an open book. She doesn't really have anything to hide. While it's reassuring, I'm not sure about it . . . there's no mystery."

I don't know what to say, so I just watch him. He has gotten something back, he seems more confident. I want to ask him more about the day my mother died, and tell him I found the cuff link, but I know this isn't the time.

"If you see her in the morning, don't be alarmed, okay?"

"Okay. Did you tell Tile?"

"No. I thought maybe you could talk to him about it. He really looks up to you."

"No problem."

He kisses me on my forehead and leaves the room. I reopen the email and wonder why Daria wants to hang out with me. I figure it won't hurt, especially if we meet in public. But doesn't she have people her own age to shop with?

When I see Elise in the morning, I notice that she looks different. Loosened. It's strange having her in my kitchen, spilling sugar on the counter and not cleaning it up. She smiles at me from behind her coffee mug and suddenly I feel transparent.

"So, are you like, moving in now?"

She laughs and shakes the hair out of her eyes. "The U-Haul is outside."

Good, I think, *she has a sense of humor.* Tile runs in and grabs the toast I made for him and jumps into the breakfast nook. I gave him a little prep talk about Elise last night, but he barely seems to notice her.

When she leaves the kitchen, I clean up her spilled sugar and rinse her mug out with extra-hot water. Tile watches me curiously.

"So that's Dad's new girlfriend?"

"I think so. Do you like her?"

He's quiet for a moment, then says, "We made cookies yesterday."

"That's good. I think it's right for Dad to have a new friend around."

"How many times a day do you think about Mom?"

He's serious now. It's frightening, these moments when he looks like an adult and has so much truth in his eyes. Completely exposed.

"Five, maybe more depending on the day. What about you?"

"A thousand," he says, as if it's a single-digit number.

"Well, I bet you wherever she is, every time you think about her she feels it in some way."

"No she doesn't. She's dead." Here are the adult eyes again. I feel myself caving in, like I could just start sobbing. I'm glad to actually feel things again, but it's almost easier not to. I give him a hug. He squeezes back, and he smells so pure and clean that for a moment I think, *He's going to be all right. We are all going to be all right.*

I meet Daria in the park and she has on a short black skirt and another thin sweater the color of blood, like her lipstick. She sits down next to me on a bench and sighs.

"You live around here, right?"

"Very close," I say.

She puts her hand on my thigh and says, "Well, let's move."

She takes me to Victoria's Secret and buys me a "starter" bra. I am not even embarrassed because she has this way about her, like everything is natural. Then we go to H&M and she buys me a pink hoodie. I don't usually wear pink, but being with Daria, I feel like the possibilities are endless. She even eats pretzels from the street vendors. We get two, draw thin lines of mustard on them, and sit at a bus stop. She asks me about boys and I start telling her about Oliver. His curly hair, the music, and the way he looked at me at the dry cleaner.

"You need a plan of attack," she says, wiping mustard from the corner of her mouth.

"Attack?"

"You know, a plan."

"I really want to watch him play."

"Good. Tell him you are writing an essay for school on classical music. And you'd like to sit in on his rehearsal for research purposes."

I don't have the heart to tell Daria this is a dumb idea, so I just shrug. A bus pulls up and the driver smiles at us.

"Or . . . what if you just ask him, flat out?"

If someone had said this to me a month ago I would never have considered it, but I'm feeling strangely empowered after finding Mom's phone. "Yeah, why not?"

"Okay, but here's the thing. Act aloof, like it was just something that popped into your mind. Never give too much away."

What is it with adults and their secrets? I start watching the people walk by: a businessman, a skater kid, an old lady. I realize they all have secrets, hidden like small stones in their pockets.

"What should I wear?"

"Wear the hoodie I got you, and your favorite jeans. It's very important that you wear your favorite jeans."

She gets a call on her cell phone and talks for a minute while I finish my pretzel.

"I've got to run downtown for a go-see."

I know this term, as my mother was always on go-sees. It's where a designer or a photographer gives you a quick look to see if you're right for a shoot or a runway show. Daria throws half of her pretzel in the trash and kisses me on both cheeks.

"You have my cell, right? Let me know how it goes with Cello Boy."

"Okay." As she walks away I say, "Thanks for everything." She turns around and waves her hand like it was nothing. I realize I never got to ask her about the cuff link, whether it might belong to Benjamin. Maybe the next message will lead me there.

When I get home, I go into my room and put on the bra and the hoodie. I walk over to the window and look for Oliver. He's not there, but my heart still picks up. Tomorrow is the day I turn fifteen, and I'm going to ask Oliver if I can watch him play.

CHAPTER 9

QUINCE

When I come downstairs in the morning, there are balloons everywhere, and my dad and Tile have made a giant sign that says MOON IS QUINCE!! There's a huge pile of chocolate chip pancakes. They sing "Happy Birthday," and at the end, Tile runs up and hugs me.

I'm not in the mood for pancakes, but they're so sweet to have done all this that I start to serve myself one. Tile already has chocolate on his rocket-ship pajamas. My dad brings me orange juice and says, "A fine vintage."

I take a sip and look through the kitchen window. I can just barely see Oliver walking out of his house. He sits down on his stoop like he's waiting for someone. Something tells me that this is the time.

I run upstairs and put my hair up, then down, then up again. Wearing it up makes me look older, closer to

Oliver's sixteen. I return to the kitchen and announce, "Be right back!" before my dad can even do anything.

It's a perfect spring day, and I descend the stairs slowly and casually, like Daria would. I walk over to Oliver, who is twirling an unpeeled banana around in his hands.

"Hi," I say.

"Hey."

"I'm fifteen." *Oh my god. What a dorky thing to say.* He smiles anyway and holds out his hand.

"I'm Oliver. Nice to meet you, Fifteen."

I giggle a little, sit down, and ask him what he's up to.

"Waiting for my mom. She's taking me to a play."

"Cool," I say, as aloof as possible.

A siren goes off and he looks down the street. I use the time to glance at his face. His skin looks pillow soft. I decide to forge on.

"Hey, do you think I could listen to you play sometime?"

"You already do."

I can feel my face heat up. He knows I listen from my room. *Duh.*

"Well, yes, but I mean, in person."

His driver pulls up, and his mom waves out of the back window. He stands up to leave. "What do I get out of the deal?"

I don't know what to say, but he's almost at the car, so I need to think of something fast. "Cookies. I'll bring cookies."

He turns around and smiles.

"Just bring yourself. Five o'clock."

"Cool. See you then."

The car pulls away and I look up at our kitchen window and see Tile and my father, apparently watching the entire time. Suddenly, I feel very private. I am fifteen and there are so many things that will have to change.

Before I retrieve the next message, I decide to go to the scene of the accident. Perhaps there will be something there, some clue I can use later on.

I take the subway down to the East Village, where every day is like Halloween. There's a different set of rules for everything. Goths, punks, gays, bookworms, schizophrenics, fashionistas, cooks, hoodlums—they all coexist together, which to me is thrilling but also dangerous. I stand on the corner of Fifth Street and Second Avenue and stare at the pavement. My mother was hit by a taxicab right here. As the taxis go by, I wonder what it felt like for her. Did she feel what it was like to fly?

When I got home from camp after finding out, still in a kind of numb haze, I fell asleep on the couch sitting up. In the middle of the night I woke to a low moaning sound. I walked upstairs to find my father packing all her things. I went downstairs for water and read part of the police report he had accidentally left on the kitchen counter. I only got to read the first paragraph before he came down, concerned that I wasn't sleeping. It had mentioned the location, and that the driver of the taxicab was not intoxicated.

She died on this street. She was wearing a dress.

Okay, it's time for another message. I walk north and take my mother's cell phone out once more, press 1 for the next voice mail. It's my father, and he sounds sedated.

"I . . . I . . . Just call me, will you?"

I stop as all the pedestrians swerve around me. Suddenly, I feel like this is all wrong. Maybe I shouldn't be listening to these messages. Maybe I should rejoin the Rachels and obsess over *Twilight*. But in spite of my doubts, I still feel like there's something missing, like a restaurant sign with one letter dark. If I can finish spelling the word maybe the story will make sense.

I feel exhausted. I go uptown to my mother's studio with the intention of opening the "Luna" folder, but end up falling asleep on her still-naked mattress. I wake up at four-thirty and rush home to shower.

When I knock on Oliver's door, the housekeeper answers. She has chopsticks in her hair and a turquoise necklace on. She looks like the type of person who's always happy. I wonder if she's high on something. She calls Oliver's name and he appears, seconds later, like he was waiting in the wings.

His room is spotless and lined in dark, highly polished wood. The ornate moldings remind me of a castle. He walks over and sits down at the cello. He picks up the bow and looks at it, as if searching for an imperfection. Then he starts the first note, low and smooth, seemingly somber, until the song goes high and playful. Is he improvising?

I sit down on the floor while he plays and all I can think is *Don't ever let this end.* I lose track of time and eventually lie on the floor and close my eyes. When he finishes, I hear his feet scuffle over to the bed, which creaks when he plops himself down. I open my eyes and sit up, and he's staring at me with a half smile, almost sinister.

"You play really well."

"I'm performing a concert in Paris this summer. There were five hundred kids and eight were chosen." He manages to say this matter-of-factly, without bragging.

"That's so cool," I say.

"So what about you, Fifteen, you play any instruments?"

"No. But I sing sometimes."

"Cool, sing something."

He's expecting me to just sing something right now?

I shake my head but he keeps staring at me. So I sing the first four lines of "Somewhere Over the Rainbow" and he closes his eyes, like I did for him. I take liberties with it, making it my own version. After, he sits up and says, "That was beautiful."

It's weird hearing a boy describe something as beautiful, but I know Oliver isn't like other boys. He is his own species, like me.

"Sing it again, and I'll play along."

He's so disarming that I'm not even nervous. While I sing he plays notes along with me, sometimes harmonizing intuitively, as if he already knows my take on the song.

When we finish, we both giggle a little, and his mother comes in. The only way I can describe her is *tight*. Her face is tight, her clothes are tight, and her hair is pulled back so tight it looks like she's in pain. But when she smiles, I can see she's very attractive.

"Would you two like a snack?"

"No thank you," we both say in unison.

She smiles again and gives me a pointed look.

"Well, dinner in an hour, Ollie. Would you like to join us, dear?"

"It's okay, maybe another time, thank you," I say.

When she leaves he says, "You're better off—it's her night to cook and it's usually some healthy stuff, like macaroni and cheese, but the cheese isn't really cheese."

This strikes me as funny, so I laugh a little.

It's clear that our rendezvous is over. He's putting his cello away and looks a little distracted. I walk up to him and shake his hand, like an adult.

"Thanks," I say.

"Don't mention it."

As I'm leaving, he calls for me and I turn around.

"I'm sorry about your mother. She was always so nice to me, and she seemed so mysterious. Sometimes I wished she was mine."

He looks vulnerable. I cannot believe I do this, but I

walk up to him and say, "If she was, then we'd be brother and sister, and that would mean I couldn't kiss you."

This time *he* blushes.

Instead of kissing him, I touch part of his curls, and they are even softer than I imagined. *How does a boy have such incredible hair?*

"Bye, Oliver."

"See you around, Fifteen."

CHAPTER 10

THE FIRST SHOT

My father comes to my door, ready to go bowling. I feel like our birthday ritual, which I have always loved, has to be put to bed.

"Can we see a movie instead?"

He looks defeated, but slides his glasses up his nose and says, "Sure, what's your fancy? Comedy? Thriller?"

"Romance, actually."

We have our driver drop us off downtown. As we wait in line at the cinema, I keep thinking about Oliver's pillow hair and soft eyes. My dad senses it.

"So, you think you and Oliver will go steady?"

I've never really talked to my dad about boys. Ever since the fifth grade when Bradford Noble tried to kiss me on the playground and I kicked him in the crotch, he never really pursued it. Maybe he thinks I'm a lesbian.

"No, but I like his sister," I say.

"He doesn't have a sister."

"Bummer."

We sit on the side aisle. Even my dad, who has a strong aversion to Hugh Grant, seems to be enjoying himself. I remember being younger and thinking the things that happened in movies were possible. I guess sometimes they are, but this movie is a modern fairy tale where dreams effortlessly come true. Because of my recent crush on Oliver, I am completely drawn in to the point of dorkiness. I even cry.

After, we wait in line to go into John's pizza, where everyone sits inches apart from one another and it's so loud we have to yell. It has an opposite effect and calms me, being submerged in a cacophony of sounds. It takes me just as far from my life as Hugh Grant did.

In the movie, the bad guy lost the girl. Watching my father eat his pizza folded like a cone, I wonder why it had to happen to him. He's the stable one, always telling the truth and giving all of himself, just a really strong, good man. I look at all the people eating together, many of them happy couples. Always something there to remind me.

When we get home, Dad stops us short and says, "Hey! Since you darted off earlier I never got to give you your present!"

He reaches into the bottom cabinet and pulls out a large box that was obviously professionally wrapped—it's too elaborate. Tile comes barreling in and sits on a stool. Presents bring a crowd.

"Wait!" Tile says. "Me first." He reaches into his pocket and takes out a small manila envelope. "Like Uncle Richard says, the best presents come in envelopes."

I open it up and pull out a small white index card. In green marker it says, *This certificate entitles you to one foot rub and two homemade cookies, courtesy of Tile Clover.* I smile and lean over, kiss him on his forehead.

My dad looks impatient, so I open the box and cannot believe what I see. It's a vintage camera, the kind I've always wanted, where you stick your head under the black fabric to take a shot. It has the original manual, and the wood is the color of a plum. The film is the size of a slice of bread. It's exquisite.

I hug him and he looks at me, blushing.

"You've always had an eye. Ever since you were this high." He puts his hand to his knee. He's right. Since third grade I've loved taking pictures. And with the exception of the collage I did with the Rachels, not of people. Mostly of buildings and textures, and strange things in nature. Natural composition that somehow looks unnatural. I never really showed them to people, but my dad's entire office is covered with my life's work, wall to wall. Some are pretty cool, but most are really amateurish. People say the onslaught of digital photography diminished the romance of the art, but even though it's dated, I will always love the idea of actual film. I used to use my dad's old Kodachrome and he even built me a darkroom, but I barely use it anymore. I got sucked into the whole Photoshop thing. But now that I have this camera, I'm sure I'll be using the film again. And I'm so grateful I want to crush him with love.

"I'm gonna go set it up!"

In my room I unfold the tripod and screw on the camera, then focus it across the street. Oliver's light is on. I wait for a whole twenty minutes until he comes to the window, and take my first shot.

CHAPTER 11

THE HAPPY FACE

In the morning Tile gives me my foot massage. Even though it's way too early for dessert, I eat the cookies. He acts like he's a professional masseur. After he's done with the left foot, he sighs. "Are you gonna marry Oliver from across the street?"

"Better. We're going to elope. To Fiji."

"Where's that?"

"It's an island."

"Are there coconuts?"

"A ton."

"Well, be careful because a thousand and nine people a year die from coconuts falling on their heads." He starts doing this thing that I love, where he rolls his knuckles down my soles. I tip my head back and finish the cookie.

Before he leaves he turns around at my door and stands in this crooked way that means he's going to get serious.

"Something about Mom's death was fishy."

I sit upright.

"What?"

"Don't make me repeat it," he says, and shuts the door.

Some kids are brought up on Nickelodeon and Dr. Seuss, but Tile started reading my dad's scripts at age six and memorizing all the juiciest lines. In this case, he read my mind, 'cause ever since finding that cuff link it's like this little seed I don't know if I want to plant.

I go and find him in his room, throwing his dirty clothes into his hamper.

"Why do you think that?" I ask.

"Do the math," he says.

Okay, he's definitely been reading Dad's scripts.

"Right," I say, smiling as I turn away. That's Tile trying to be dramatic, pretending he knows something.

Back in my room, I tell myself it's now or never. Eventually I'm going to have to give Mom's phone back, so I might as well continue. But slowly.

I lock my door, breathe in, and grab Mom's phone.

I have been deleting them as I go, so as not to leave a trace, and there are four more.

"To listen to your messages, press one."

"Hi, this is Angela, calling from Butter restaurant. I believe someone in your party left a personal item; please come by any time after four p.m. Tuesday through Sunday to retrieve it. Thank you."

I immediately go online and look up the restaurant. It's

only three blocks from where my mother was hit. My heart rate speeds up. Did she go there the night she died?

I go into my father's office and he puts down the script he's reading when he sees the look on my face, which I try to erase.

"Can I ask you something?"

"Sure, Moon, shoot."

"I know you weren't with Mom the night she died, and every time I asked you, you avoided the question. But I really have to know. What was she doing?"

He adjusts his glasses and looks out the window before turning to me.

"She had gone to dinner with Maria, her yoga teacher. Moon, we've been through this. . . ."

"You just kept saying the details didn't matter, that she was gone. I only knew the intersection from the police report. I asked a lot and you never told me who she was with."

"Well, I did now."

My mother took yoga religiously, but only this particular class that was a combination of techniques. I went with her once and was embarrassed to run into Ms. Gray there. Something about seeing your teacher in real life is unnerving.

"So tell me, how does it feel to be fifteen?"

"Weird," I say, and go back to my room.

I grab my hoodie, my keys, and my MetroCard and leave without telling anyone. On the subway down to

Astor Place, I notice a Hispanic girl about my age looking at me intently, as if I have something she wants. My pink hoodie? I give her a wave and she smiles, embarrassed. Then I notice a woman at the end of the car, her back to me, reading while slightly curled around the silver pole. Her hair is the exact length and color of my mother's. As we rumble through the tunnel I walk closer, losing my balance a few times. I feel a strange magnetism, and as I am pulled closer I can even smell her. The train pulls into the station and I reach out to touch her, slowly, and wonder if I'm going crazy. Suddenly she twists her long neck and it's someone with the shape of my mother's face but completely different features. She looks at me like she understands, then gazes at her own feet, walking away. Until the next stop I hold on to the pole exactly where she did and close my eyes. When I get out of the subway, the fresh air feels good.

Butter is closed but I can see someone mopping the floor, and I keep tapping on the window until he finally opens the big glass door just a crack.

"What is it?"

"I left something here, it's really important," I say.

He shuts the door and holds up his hand.

It starts to rain. Two guys whistle at me as they go by and I give them the finger. I don't think I've ever done that before. *What's happening to me?*

A man with white hair in a crisp suit comes to the door and smiles, lets me in.

"Hi there, what is it you left behind?"

Shit. What am I supposed to say that won't make me seem like a lunatic?

"I'm not sure."

That pretty much did it.

"Excuse me?"

"Well, here's the deal. My mother told me to get what she left here but she didn't tell me what it was. If I could just . . ."

He walks over to the hostess stand and pulls out a black box with no top. I peek over the lid and see a watch, a pair of sunglasses, two sets of keys, and one more thing, glistening in the corner. I know immediately it's what I am looking for. One cuff link, made to look like a theater mask. The happy face.

CHAPTER 12

AKA DIANE

I race to the subway to get uptown, then literally sprint across the park. When I get back to my room I frantically search for the other cuff link that I found in Mom's studio, to make sure they're a pair. *Maria wouldn't wear cuff links.* Was someone else at dinner with them? Or . . . did my father just lie to me?

I'm staring in disbelief when my father peeks his head around the door. I close my fists around the cuff links and put my hands behind my back. For a second, I feel like a magician.

"Everything okay?" he asks.

No, no, it's not okay. Was Mom having an affair?

"Yes, fine. I'm going to take my new camera out to the street."

"Good idea," he says. "Need help?"

I can't remember the last time my father showed

interest in what I was doing. After the accident he was the king of wallowing, living in a haze of his own grief. How has he made such a turnaround? Just from hanging out with the E-word? It's like he's another person altogether. "I can handle it, thanks."

After he leaves, I decide I need to distract myself from the phone and the messages and whatever they might be revealing. I hide the cuff links in an old pair of shoes and call Daria. It takes me a whole horrifying minute to explain who I am.

"Yes! How's the bra working out?"

"Great. Thank you again. But I have a non-bra-related question for you. I know you're like, a big model and everything, but would you sit for me? I got this new vintage camera and I've been taking pictures my whole life but never of people, so I want to try. It may just be parts of you, not like, posing or anything."

"Sure. I'm at the MoMA finishing up a coffee. Be there in twenty."

"Now? Excellent." I tell her which park entrance to meet at.

As I set my camera up on the cobblestone walkway bordering the park, people stop and look at it. I still can't believe it's mine—it's so cool! I look around for any sketchy-looking people who might try to run off with it.

When Daria arrives, she sits down on a nearby bench and lights a cigarette. I leave the camera where it is and join her.

"Is that your real name, Daria?"

"No, it's Diane. I had an agent once tell me that Diane doesn't screw the camera, Daria does. Total creep. I do like Daria, though."

"Me too, but today you're going to be Diane."

She smiles. "I grew up total white trash, at least after we came to America. My mom used to make casseroles, the ones with crushed potato chips on top? We'd eat it for a week. Now I live in a five-thousand-square-foot Brooklyn loft and hardly ever fly commercial."

"Wow."

"My brother runs a landscaping company in Hackensack, where my parents live. He makes forty grand a year, and I make four hundred. When I try to get him something nice, all he ever wants is a case of beer—domestic, no less!"

"Are you Swedish?"

"Latvian."

I feel naive for thinking I had pegged her. She seems to have a lot of layers. I'm glad I'm going to photograph her. She puts her cigarette out in her coffee cup.

"People think being a model is so glamorous, but it's not. Have you read your mother's book?"

"Only parts. I'm not supposed to till I'm eighteen."

"It's humiliating, really. You go in for like, some huge spread in *VF*, and you line up and they walk by and sniff you like animals, rape you with their eyes, tapping the ones they don't want on the shoulder, until there's like three of you left and you're sweating, and—"

"Do they ever make you sleep with them?"

"That's prostitution, honey, it's illegal. But sometimes, girls do it to rise in the ranks. Then there are ones who don't really take any crap. I think your mother was like that. I'm learning. I used to do sportswear and catalogues and now I'm doing Gucci and Calvin."

"How did you first get into it?"

She looks off into the distance as if caught in a memory. Then a flash of shame washes over her face.

"I had a crush on this boy in seventh grade. He was like, half my height at the time." She giggles and turns toward me, folding one of her lanky legs under the other. "He had one of those horrible ferret things. He called it Madge. I'm not sure why I loved him so much. I think it was because I saw him as this shapeless form that I could mold into something that would be only mine. He was so . . . malleable. Anyway, I was at his house one day and we were watching some supercheesy movie, and his father came in and started staring at me. It was kind of creepy."

A homeless person walks by, having an argument with himself, while a mother pulls her pigtailed daughter out of his way.

"Then what happened?"

"He told me that I had elegant features. Can you imagine? Saying that to your twelve-year-old son's girlfriend? But something about it was right, like his intentions were innocent. I've never felt more alive than at that moment. As it turned out, he was the super for the building that then housed the Click Agency. He got me a meeting and the rest is history."

"What happened to the boy?"

Her skin blanches for a second and she frowns.

"Someone at school killed Madge and he never was the same. He ended up going to a special school. I hear he's a veterinarian now, if you can believe it."

"With a ferret specialty?"

She gives me a warm look, widening her eyes, and I notice her eyelashes seem to go on for miles.

"You . . . you're really beautiful. Hang on. Stay there."

I get the camera ready and shoot her, from the chin down, sitting on the bench in all black, knobby knees bare between her high socks and short skirt. I click and smile.

Next, I have her walk through the frame several times. I know the camera isn't advanced enough to capture motion, but it might be an interesting blur. She has on a midnight blue satin jacket and I ask her to swing it around a few times. After I take the rest of the shots in the roll, I pack up the camera and we sit back down.

Daria puts out her hand and says, "That'll be two thousand dollars, please."

"How about an ice cream sandwich?"

"That works."

As we walk toward the group of street vendors and bike cabs, I pull the cuff links out of my pocket and show them to her.

"Ever seen these?"

She looks at them quizzically and says, "No."

I am not totally convinced by her answer.

"Do you think Benjamin—"

"Where'd you get those?"

"Two different places."

"Did you steal them?"

"Not exactly."

We get our ice cream sandwiches and continue walking. I slip the cuff links back into my pocket. "Do you know if Benjamin and my mom ever, you know . . ."

She laughs. "No, I don't know."

"Forget it."

"Benjamin's gay, sweetheart."

"Oh." *So that rules him out.*

We make it to my stoop and I ask her if she wants to come in.

"No. I've got to get home to pack for Paris. I've been spending a lot of time there because of my *Elle* contract. But you should come back and visit sometime. I'm across the hall from Benjamin, number four. Bring the photographs. I'm back Thursday."

"Okay, thanks again . . . you rock," I add, immediately regretting it. I watch her walk away and try to picture myself with her gait, her easy stare, her way of pushing herself through the world, as if nothing could stop her.

CHAPTER 13

DIGGING FOR COLE

I gather the film and materials and head down to the basement. Tile tries to follow me but I remind him that there are too many chemicals.

"What, it's PG-13 down there or something?"

"You could say that, yes. Well, it's R, but Dad lets me 'cause I know what I'm doing."

"Who was that lady?"

"A model. Actually, a friend."

"A friend of Mom's?"

"No. Don't you have homework?"

"Yeah, math tables I can do in my sleep. Whose phone is that?"

Oh my god, he's seen Mom's phone.

"It's my friend's. She left it."

"No it's not, she had an iPhone. I saw it."

"Tile, it's my other friend's."

"Something's not adding up," he says.

I roll my eyes. "Why don't you go read another one of Dad's scripts."

"Okay, but tell me who—"

I shut the door and descend the stairs.

As the pictures develop, I crouch outside the darkroom and realize that though Tile is clueless, he may be right. It's not adding up. Now that I know the cuff link is not Benjamin's, it could be anyone's, and I really need to find out whose. I take out Mom's phone and hope the next message will shed some light.

Beep.

Clearly someone called her without knowing it, 'cause it's a long message of people talking in what seems to be a bar. Clinking glasses, some laughter, and what sounds like stools scraping across a floor. There's a male voice toward the end. He's mumbling and shaking a glass of ice. Then another voice that's amplified by a microphone, greeting the crowd, some applause. It sounds like he says, "Welcome to the Laugh House."

I save this one, 'cause I may need to hear more. I take the photographs out of the solution and hang them to dry. Back in my room I Google *Laugh House* and nothing in Manhattan comes up. I listen to the message again and try *Laugh Lounge* instead. It shows up on the Lower East Side.

I go back to the basement and look at the pictures.

Obviously, I still need to get the hang of the camera. Everything's manual, so I was really just guessing. But there are two pictures that stand out: the silhouette of Oliver in his window, and the one of Daria sitting on the bench. Oliver looks like a ghost and Daria looks like someone dangerous. I decide to give Oliver the picture, the first one taken by my camera.

I walk across the street with the photograph turned toward my chest, protecting it from the natural elements. His housekeeper answers again. She doesn't look as happy this time, so I give her an extra-bright smile. She points upstairs and shakes her head, indicating that Oliver isn't there. I hand her the photograph.

"Could you give that to him?"

She nods, takes the picture, and shuts the door. I look at Mom's phone: 3:30. It takes me two trains to find the F, which I take to Second Avenue, near Ludlow. People have this fear of New York being a dangerous city, but I've never felt unsafe. Today it's all hipsters and slackers, smoking and slapping each other on the back, and African nannies with pale babies in designer strollers. Ludlow Street used to be rough, I do know that. My mom told me she once went to an up-and-coming designer's place on Stanton, to see about doing a Milan show, and heard shots fired next door. But that was twenty years ago, when the KFC had bulletproof glass.

The place looks like it just opened, and there's a bartender in her thirties, from Korea or maybe Japan. She smiles at me and I smile back, trying to act nonchalant.

"I have a...strange request. I think someone accidentally called me from here and I wondered if you could—"

The phone rings behind the bar and she keeps looking at me as she answers it. I suddenly feel misguided and out of place. *What am I doing here?*

She puts down the phone and sighs, walks over to me and waits for me to go on.

"Could you maybe listen to the voice on this message and just tell me if you recognize it?"

"Why don't you sit," she says, and starts wiping the counter with a dingy towel. Something in her sees my desperation, even though I'm trying to hide it. She pours me a Sprite.

"Wait a minute," she says. "How do you know they called from here?"

"A comic gets introduced and says welcome to the Laugh Lounge."

She looks at me like I'm really clever.

"Okay, give it to me."

I find the message and hand the phone over. As she listens, I study her face. She smiles a little, and then opens her mouth like she's going to sing.

"That's Cole, one of our regulars. You're right! Go, Nancy Drew."

"I prefer James Bond, but I'll take what I can get."

She gives me back the phone and a look of pleasure falls over her pale, angular face. "You aren't going to stalk him or anything?"

"No, just boil his bunny."

She squints and her face becomes something else entirely, a feral cat with wounded eyes. Then she's instantly back to being pleasant. "Cole . . . hang on."

She turns to the cash register and pulls a picture off a bulletin board covered with snapshots of smiling customers. She hands it to me, and I look down at an attractive man my mother's age having what looks like a scotch at that very bar.

"That's him," she says.

I hold this picture close. He looks shiny and clean, blond hair slicked back. When she turns her head, I secretly place it under a bar napkin.

"When does he come in here?"

She looks above my head, toward the light from the street.

"He used to come all the time. The other bartender likes to take snapshots of our biggest customers. But he hasn't come in a long time, actually. Maybe a year."

She busies herself behind the bar for a while and I sip my drink. When I get up to leave she shakes my hand, like I'm a full-grown adult. I steal the picture and she pretends not to notice.

Back on the subway I study Cole in the photograph. He has on a black sport coat. He looks eager. I glance up and notice that everyone on the entire subway car is reading, trying to transport themselves away. I pull out Mom's phone and search through the contacts. Catherine, Cate, Charles . . . *Cole.*

It's lame when you try so hard to get what you want, and then when you get it, you realize you need something else even harder to get. I really don't want to believe that my mother was cheating, but something is telling me to keep following my instincts. I mean, what if finding her phone was a sign? And speaking of signs, I now know there were others, besides when I found her talking on the phone in the bathtub. It's like when you love someone so much you are blind to their flaws.

I went to one of her photo shoots once, in the Meatpacking District. I remember she had nothing on, but there were balloons covering her private parts. There was a man in the picture with real snakes around his neck who freaked me out. It was an ad for Diesel jeans that ended up everywhere. There were trailers, and Mom had her own. I was waiting outside with Tile, and through the makeshift window I heard kissing sounds. At the time I just thought it was one of the makeup artists, the gay guys she was always kissing. Now I wonder if it was someone else. But if she was really fooling around, why would she do it with Tile and me so close by?

As I approach my building, I run into my dad on the street. He looks angry.

"Hey, listen. I saw you coming out of the subway. What's our rule on this?"

I realize I'm still holding the photograph. I try to subtly slip it into my back pocket. I start to stammer a little, until—I swear—Oliver comes out of nowhere, spinning his book bag.

"She was with me," he says, "and my housekeeper. See?" He points to his housekeeper walking up the steps across the way. I nod my head as if it's perfectly natural that I'd be traveling on the subway with Oliver and his housekeeper.

"All right, but next time tell me where you're going. You coming up?"

"In a sec."

He leaves us there, and Oliver keeps swinging his bag and looking at me.

"Thanks for the picture," he says. "It's really macabre."

"Not really what I was shooting for, but you're welcome."

"No, in a good way."

"Okay."

He kisses me on the cheek, easy, like he planned it. Then he pushes up the sleeve of my hoodie, writes his phone number on the underside of my forearm, and gently slides my sleeve back down.

"Later, Fifteen."

I watch him run up his stairs and disappear behind the giant wooden door. Then I roll up my sleeve and make sure it's still there, that I didn't dream it.

CHAPTER 14

SIGNS

Tile, Dad, Elise, and I have dinner in the dining room, which we haven't used since Mom died. It's something Elise made, and the only way I can describe it is *stew*. Even though I think I like her, it feels weird having her in my house, and the fact that Tile loves the stew is making me burn with anxiety. It's not about the stew, of course, but about everything I've learned over the past week, and the question still swimming in my head. Was my mom having an affair? It sounds corny, but for as long as I can remember, when I picture my parents in memories, they're smiling. They had their own separate lives, for sure, but when they were together they were happy. The only time I ever sensed something was off was one night when I'd come back from Rachel One's eleventh birthday party. I heard whimpering, and opened the door to the powder room to find my mom on the floor, her gown splayed around her like a parachute. She was crying, and when she saw me she didn't stop, it just got worse. I asked her what was wrong and she kept saying, "I'm fine, Luna, I'm fine."

I got her into bed and went back downstairs into the kitchen to get some water. My dad was sitting at the table with an empty glass in his hand. He wasn't crying, but he looked fallen.

"Hey, Moon."

"Hi. What's going on?"

He waved his hand. "Minor bumps in the road. Nothing to be startled about."

"Okay." As I left, he cleared his throat really loud so I turned around.

"You know that no matter what, your mother and I, we will always love you and Tiley."

I remember thinking this wasn't something my father would say. Way too Hallmark Channel. But he meant it, and I told myself it *would* be okay. Now, watching Elise reach for another scoop of her stew, I wonder if it ever was.

All through the next day, my first day back at school, I make sure the number doesn't fade, protecting it with my long-sleeve sweater. It's time for *me* to carry a secret.

Between fourth and fifth periods I see the two Rachels

in the bathroom. They're doing their lipstick and looking totally put-together.

Six months ago I was like one of those people who walk along the side of highways. Lost, and maybe a little crazy. Now I feel on track, but I'm not sure exactly where I'm headed.

The first time I actually cried after Mom's death was at the end of the reception following the funeral. Most people had gone, but there was a group of women huddled in the den, looking at some magazine that my mother was in. I crept up behind them without them noticing, to get a glimpse of the page they had suddenly stopped at. It was a girl my age, dressed in short shorts and what looked like a high-fashion sports bra.

A few of them gasped and one woman said, with unveiled disdain, "Can you imagine the mother who'd let her daughter out in something like that?"

I have never been drunk, but I imagine what I felt was similar. A deep gravity consumed me, and I fell to the floor in slow motion, crouching behind the couch. Someone called from the kitchen and all the women got up to leave. Then I felt a sharp pain in my stomach, like I had been punched, and I literally couldn't breathe. My eyes became rivers and everything blurred.

Eventually Rachel One came in. She sat down next to me but didn't touch me.

"You know what's really sad? Your mother was the coolest—she wasn't really like a mom, you know? My mother is like an android."

Leave it to Rachel One to make it about her. She does have a heart in there somewhere, but her narcissism is intense.

"She was a mom. She was my mom," I said.

My breath caught a couple more times, and Rachel just adjusted her position, then her bracelets, and then her hair.

"Anyway, see you in school."

She started to walk away but then turned around and reached out her manicured hand to help me up. She was the first girl in school to have earrings, be able to wear lip gloss, and get highlights. But if that's all there is to strive for, what a sad existence. The fakeness of it all made me hold back another fit of tears. She helped me up and I just stood there, studying the empty room. Everything—the curve of the couch, the droopy plant, the billowy curtains—looked different. It was a house without a mom.

My father was upstairs, and Tile was long gone with my grandmother, and no one else was in the house. It seemed so hard to comprehend. There was no order in anything, only swirling thoughts, until one memory settled itself, perhaps one of the earliest ones I had. It was my sixth birthday party, and everyone was waiting for me to take a bite of the "cake," which was actually pie. I had one of those spastic moments when your body just acts without messages from your mind. I flipped the piece of cherry pie onto my white blouse—of course I was wearing white. After it happened I stood like a stunned animal, and everyone looked on the verge of bursting into laughter, including the parents. Time seemed to stretch and I remember feeling my head about to explode, then *bam*—my mother dips her hand into her pie and smears it onto her dress, just like that. The pressure in my head evaporated, and before I knew it, everyone was putting cherry pie on each other. Yes, it sounds like a dumb movie but it wasn't. It was my mother, and her quirky way of handling the situation. She had my back and always protected me, like a lioness with her cub.

So there I was, alone, in a room filled with crumpled-up napkins and leftover drinks. I smelled one of them and could tell it was scotch. I'm not sure why they say alcohol numbs pain. All it did for me was sting my throat and make me want to brush my teeth. Still, I would have reached for anything at that moment. Anything that would take me back to being six, when the worst thing that could happen was staining my clothes with cherry pie.

Now, Rachel One looks at me in her pompous way, then shoos everyone out of the bathroom. I'm glad I'm wearing my blue dress. Even though I'm not really proud of it, I miss her.

"Is that the Marc Jacobs?" she asks.

"Yes."

"How are you?"

Could you have asked me that at the funeral?

"Okay."

"You look much better."

"Thanks."

I don't really want to care this much about Rachel One, but I find myself smiling at her like a complete dork.

"I have a new cell, call me, we'll catch up." She hands me a pale pink card with her number written in baby blue cursive.

"Sure."

Janine comes in as Rachel leaves and makes a sound that disapproves of me. She points at the card.

"Back in the clique?" she says, shaking her hair out, then refastening it with a red scrunchie.

"Yeah. Whoopee."

"The funny thing is, everyone thinks they need the Rachels' approval now, but in ten years they'll probably be in some miserable marriage popping out babies for show. Tired."

She's probably right. As she leans back a little, I notice that her breasts are way bigger than mine. I tell her a little bit about my Oliver crush. She says we should go on a double date with her and her motorcycle-riding boyfriend.

"Well, let's wait until he kisses me," I say, showing her the digits he wrote on my arm.

She runs her fingers along the numbers. "That is so romantic. He really wanted to make a mark, so to speak."

"Let's hope so," I say.

After English, Ms. Gray pulls me aside. She has on

mom jeans and a blue Gap sweater dated about ten years. Her lack of style does nothing to hold back her spirit. After my mother died, she was the only reason I even came to school. She gave me a small journal and told me that whenever I wanted to speak to my mom, I should write my thoughts in it. I never wrote anything, but I still have it, a reminder that someone cared. For three weeks she was the only person I'd talk to. She has this gift for being able to make every single person in her class feel like they're extraordinary.

I show her some of my photographs.

"This is your calling!" she says in a stage whisper.

"I got this vintage camera, Sands Hunter. It's amazing."

"That is wonderful! Can you bring it in to show the class?"

"But it has nothing to do with English."

"I'll make an exception. C'mon, it'll be great."

"Okay," I say. "I will. But I had a question. You know when I saw you at my mom's yoga class that time?"

"Yes, dear, what is it?"

"When does Maria teach?"

"Wednesdays and Fridays at four, why?"

"Nothing, I just want to take her class."

Ms. Gray knows something is up and gives me a funny look. On my way out, I look back at her and she says, "I'm still here, you know. If you need anything."

"Thanks."

Janine talks all the way home but I'm not really listening. My mind is focused on what is up my sleeve.

* * *

When I get home I stare at the phone for a few minutes before dialing the numbers on my arm. His mother answers, seemingly excited that Oliver has a girl calling him. She tries to act normal but it's obvious.

"Thanks for helping me out yesterday," I say when he gets on the line.

"My pleasure. But where were you?"

"It's a long story, but that's what I called you about. I need your help. Well, sort of."

"Okay, how?"

At the risk of sounding like Tile, I say, "There's foul play."

Silence on the line. I decide to just forge on.

"I am, well, looking into my mother's death. I have her phone, and there are seven messages. I am listening to each one in order to see if I can piece it all together."

"What do you mean, 'looking into her death'?"

"I'll explain. But listen, can . . . can you come with me later? To yoga?"

More silence. I feel my heart banging against my rib cage.

"Hang on."

I hear him speaking Spanish to his housekeeper; then his breathing comes back on the line. "What time?" he says.

"Four."

The housekeeper starts talking again.

"Okay. Fifteen, I have to go. See you outside at three-thirty."

I hang up the phone. Just as my heart starts to regain its normal beat, I see the picture of Cole sitting on my desk and it hits me. I scan the photograph into my computer. Using the micro zoom in Photoshop, I magnify his wrist area. It's hard to tell what kind, but he's definitely wearing a cuff link, and it's silver.

CHAPTER 15

DEEP BREATHING

As we walk the ten blocks to the yoga studio I fill Oliver in on everything. He seems very intrigued by it all, and even though it's potentially more horrible than it already seems, I get a rush from his reaction. Before I'm finished, it looks as if he's already devising a plan.

"So why do we have to actually take the yoga class?"

"To be nonchalant."

"I like how you think, Fifteen."

The place is a huge, spotless studio overlooking Columbus Avenue. We set up our mats far enough away that it's not awkward. The fact that he looks like he's dressed for soccer practice is adorable. I'm suddenly seeing why the Rachels are so obsessed with boys. I'm thinking, as I sneak looks at him during the opening breathing, that I just never had the right one to fixate on.

Maria's tan makes me feel like an albino. The class is

superhard and we're completely drenched in sweat by the end. She doesn't recognize me until I introduce myself.

"Luna! I haven't seen you in years, you're all grown!"

I smile and turn the attention to Oliver, whose curls are flattened onto his face.

"You guys were really good. Your first time?"

"This type, yes. But I actually have a question for you."

Here's when she gets that look. The one of sympathy that I guess I should appreciate, but most of the time it makes me feel worse. She knows the question's going to be about my mother.

"Sure. Anything."

"Were you with my mother at Butter the night she died?"

Some long-haired guy quickly hugs her on his way out, sweat and all. Oliver cringes.

"No, dear, I wasn't."

Time slows down. I feel my heart drop through the floor and my throat constrict, and I want to scream, *Yes! Yes you were!* But she wasn't, which means my father lied to me. Oliver is studying his bare feet and wiggling his toes.

"Why do you ask?"

"Just curious," I say, but it comes out like a whimper. I feel pathetic.

"I haven't . . . *hadn't* seen your mother since that fundraiser on the boat. She had taken a hiatus from my class. I'm so terribly sorry, Luna."

Please don't let her hug me with the combined sweat of everyone in her class that just hugged her.

"Thank you," I say, and quickly turn away.

When we get outside, Oliver says, "I know what you need now."

He takes me to a place called the Creperie and—I'm serious—orders in French. My anger toward my father is momentarily dissolved as my teeth sink into a thin banana-chocolate crepe with melted vanilla ice cream.

"So who do you think was really with her that night?" Oliver asks as we finish our crepes.

"Well, it's obviously someone important, or my father wouldn't have lied about it."

"Right. Cole?"

"That would explain the cuff link. Will you try and find him with me?"

"This sure beats doing my scales," he says, and leaves a crisp twenty on the table.

"Was that a date?" I ask as we enter the pedestrian traffic.

"If you wanted it to be," he says.

As we walk toward home, Oliver looks at me with genuine concern.

"Do you think your mom was having an affair with this guy?"

"I'm not sure. I don't want to even go there without knowing for sure, you know?"

"Yeah. My dad was having an affair before they got

divorced. There was this woman who gave me tennis lessons. It's ridiculous how naive I was. She was practically falling all over him.

"Do you think your father was somehow involved in the accident?"

His direct questioning has a bizarre effect on me. Instead of being defensive, I am totally at ease. He grasps my hand for a minute, then uncurls his fingers to let go.

"I hadn't even thought about that, but maybe he was."

There's an old woman holding court on her stoop with two UPS guys. Oliver stops me at the corner and gives me a serious look.

"Whatever it is, Fifteen, I think it's good you are doing this. You deserve to know."

We continue in silence, and he takes my hand again, this time holding on. In the middle of all that's happening, something feels right. I let each breath go deep and relish it. When we get to my door we almost kiss, but we both become self-conscious. Instead, he puts his hand under my chin for a brief time, and I feel prettier than any Rachel in the world.

CHAPTER 16

HEAVY STUFF

I avoid my father tonight. I'm afraid of the sharp words that may hurl out of my mouth. When there's a knock on my door, I brace myself. Thankfully, it's only Tile.

"Shouldn't you be in bed?"

"Elise's here, so all the rules go out the window," Tile says with a smile.

"She is?"

"Can't you smell her? It's like, onions or something . . . ew."

"It's called patchouli."

"Pawhosit?"

For a moment I wish I were Tile's age, so immune to the hardness of things. My mother's death will affect him more as he grows older. Especially when he finds out what I'm discovering. Do I want to know more? Is there a legitimate reason why my father wouldn't tell me who was at dinner that night?

I tell Tile to get lost, and will myself to relax. I listen to my iPod for a while, music always being my chosen form of escape, then drift off to sleep.

The next day I take the entire stack of Daria photos and put them in a big envelope. My father's still with Elise, and Tile is right—all rules are off.

This time the cabdriver who gives me a ride to Greenpoint is talking very loudly into an earpiece in what I believe is Swahili. It sounds like chanting, and it has a calming effect on me.

Once again, I have the driver wait outside the building. I run up and knock on number four and Daria comes to the door in a robe, looking like she just woke up. She rolls her eyes and I tell her I'll come back another time, but she points at the portfolio.

"Those them?" she asks in a hoarse voice.

"Yeah."

She motions me in. I hand her the envelope and she opens it and pulls out my favorite one of her, from the chin down, on the bench in the park. She giggles a little and then looks at the rest. She spreads them all over the floor and at one point her robe slips, revealing part of her nipple. I look away. An entire section of her apartment is lined with cardio machines.

"Wow. You, my dear, are incredibly talented."

I don't know what to say except "Thanks."

"Listen, I've got to go back to sleep, but I have an idea. Can I keep these for now?"

"Um, okay."

"Call me on Tuesday. Go back to the city. I know I told you to come, but you're not supposed to be here, right?"

"I know, the cab's waiting. Bye."

She kisses me on both cheeks and her hair smells like apples. As she walks toward her bedroom, she scratches her butt.

On the way down the stairs I wonder not only why she wanted to keep the shots, but also why I so casually agreed.

During the cab ride back to the city, I feel good, like maybe all this is happening for a reason. But I don't get my dad lying to me. I have the driver drop me off at the Creperie, where I order an orange soda and tell myself I'm ready for the next message. What could be worse than your dad lying and your mom having an affair with someone who wears costume cuff links? I am so mad at both of them right now I almost smash the phone on the ground. Instead I take a deep breath like Ms. Gray says to do.

Beep.

"Hi, it's me. I got your email and wanted to talk in person. Heavy stuff. Call me."

I can tell immediately it's Richard, my mom's brother, the one who lives in Italy. What "heavy stuff" is he talking about?

At the funeral, Richard spoke and dressed so

eloquently, and I sat on the piano bench while his boy-friend, Julian, played, mesmerized by his long fingers. I think it was Chopin, and it struck me as beautiful but very sad. The three of us ended up in the kitchen in the morning, and I remember Richard talking in hushed tones to Julian. All I heard were the words *what killed her*. When they noticed I was there it was like time suspended for a second, and they tried to cover it up. I thought something weird was going on, but because it was such a traumatic time I never thought about it again. There were too many other things to worry about, like living the rest of my life without a mother.

When I arrive home there's that same sort of tension in the air. My father's sitting on the stairs, holding the picture of Cole and looking perplexed.

"Moon, what the hell is going on, where did you get this?"

"You went into my room?"

He stands up and holds the picture out, his hand shaking.

"I'll repeat. Where did you get this?"

I grab it out of his hand and say, "Do you know him?"

His whole body seems to be shaking now, and it scares me a little. He doesn't say anything, just keeps staring at me like I've become someone he doesn't recognize.

"Was he the person that Mom was with the night she died?"

He turns his back to me, and I realize that he's trying not to cry.

CHAPTER 17

INDISCRETION

I spend the evening in my room staring at the picture of my mother on the wall, next to one of Regina Spektor from *Rolling Stone*. My father is locked in his office, and we still haven't talked further. There are possible truths swirling around my head that I really don't want to think about. It's hard enough that my mother's not here.

To distract myself I flip through a recent issue of *New York* magazine with Drew Barrymore on the cover. I met her once at a casting for one of my father's films. She came in late, and everyone there seemed really annoyed—the producers, their assistants, even my dad, who's normally very even-keeled. I think it was because everyone was losing faith in the project. Two studios had rejected the script despite the attachment of many stars. But as it turned out, the person Drew was supposed to read with wasn't there either, so she waited in the studio next door, where I was fiddling on an upright piano. It was raining sheets, and Drew went over to the window, putting her hands up to the glass as if trying to bring back a memory. I walked up behind her and she commented on how beautiful it was. "All this rain," she said. At the time, I didn't really know who she was. She sat down on the floor and thumbed through the script. She told me that she had always wanted to work with my dad. I asked her why and she said, "I'm not sure, really. I mean, I loved *The Lazy Road*, but I also just feel like there's something about him, something exceptional."

Even though I was eight at the time, I was used to people kissing up to him. But I could tell she was for real. She wasn't saying it to try to win me over. Like I had anything to do with his casting anyway. We sat there until the rain subsided, and she told me I had mysterious eyes. I remember that distinctly, because no one had ever complimented me in that way, like you would an adult.

Most of the actors I'd met during my dad's auditions were pretty nervous. In fact, I never liked to be around them because it made *me* nervous. Drew was acting like she was in a dentist's office, waiting to get her teeth cleaned. She seemed unfazed by it all, even after she divulged her admiration of my dad and his work. I asked her why she was so calm and she smiled. She told me she'd been doing the showbiz thing for a while, and that it got her into a lot of trouble at an early age, and that she was forced to grow up fast.

"You want to know so much, you want to experience so

much, but I think it's better to let it happen gradually. At least for me, I learned way too much way too early."

Now, listening to Imogen Heap sing "Hide and Seek" on my iPod, I am wondering if I really want to know all this. I can sense that it's more than just Cole, that it may be like opening one of those Russian dolls made of painted wood that have a smaller one inside, and another, and another. The tiny little doll at the end may be the one thing that will change me forever. But it's too late. The seed has been planted, breaking out its roots, spreading the branches through me. I have to know. The lyrics in the song seem to be coming straight from my own heart:

> *Where are we?*
> *What the hell is going on?*

I knock on my father's door twice and then enter. He's staring at his screen saver, a pencil that draws characters that come to life then run away. I wonder how long he's been sitting there.

I sit down in the nook by the window.

"You have that look," he says.

I feel myself slipping, words straining to get out of my mouth. I tell him about Mom's studio and the phone, how it led to the dress, and Benjamin, and eventually Cole.

While I talk he looks at me in amazement. When I say

the name Cole, I swear there's fire in his eyes. Then his gaze suddenly turns soft and he takes a breath.

"Who is he?"

"He's a sailor," he says in a quiet voice. "Charters yachts in Europe. Has a villa near Richard's in Tuscany. I think that's where they met."

"Dad, all I ever really wanted to know was what happened when she died. You can't keep avoiding the issue. I'm old enough—"

"But why, sweetheart? There's nothing to gain from that knowledge, is there? It's best to remember her when she was alive. Yes, it was Cole who was with her, but I told you, she got hit by a taxi, I told you."

"So, Cole was having an affair with Mom?"

He looks like he might explode for a second, then says softly, "Yes, Malia, he was."

He uses my real name, which usually means the conversation is over. This is all I will get, for now. A confirmation. I try to imagine what that felt like for him, and can see in his flushed cheeks and darting eyes that it was, and is now, very hard to swallow. I feel the same way.

He clicks on the mouse and the screen saver vanishes, revealing the desktop image, a poster for his documentary. It's a picture of three old women on a bench in a park, the sky impossibly blue above their white hair. It's a movie about failed relationships—go figure. Each of the women has been married five times. My dad spent months profiling them for the film.

"How could she do that, though?"

"I asked myself the same thing."

We sit in silence for a little while.

"I'm so angry with her, but how can you be angry at someone who died?"

"It's okay to feel anger, just try not to harbor it. Try and let it go."

"Do you think you'd ever get married again?"

He looks at me seriously, to make sure my question was not for the purpose of mocking him.

"Probably not, but I've seen a lot of things happen in my lifetime I never expected."

"Yeah, me too," I say.

I still think there is something he's not telling me, so I guess I will have to find Cole and ask him myself. The more knowledge I have before hearing the next message, the better.

I walk up to him and put a hand on each of his strong shoulders. He makes an involuntary noise, implying that it feels good, so I keep them there. For several more minutes we stare at the old ladies, each one beautiful in her own way, despite the five husbands.

"Well, I'm going to sleep now," I say.

"Me too."

He shuts down the computer and we leave his office together. As I turn into my room, I hear Tile run up behind us. He follows me in.

I'm not one of those girls who can't stand their little brothers in their rooms. I do feel like my room is a sanctuary, but Tile's presence doesn't corrupt it in any way. Right now he is a welcome diversion.

"I saw your pictures."

"Tile!"

"I know I'm not supposed to go in there, but I didn't touch the chemicals. Besides, I get bored, you know. There's only so much bad TV I can handle."

I smile and wait for him to go on.

"I liked the ones of the girl. But I want to know how you met her. You don't just have friends that are, like, thirty."

I try to figure out what to say to him while he paces around.

"I met her over at Oliver's. She's actually a friend of Oliver's mom."

This white lie seems to work for the time being. He sits on his heels and draws designs in the carpet.

"What were you and Dad fighting about?"

"Nothing," I say, and go behind the closet door to change into my nightshirt.

"Seemed like something to me."

"Well, I could tell you, but then I'd have to kill you."

"Ha!" he says, delighted that I've moved into script-speak.

I get under my covers and turn off the light. The red night-light in the shape of a train makes our faces look sinister. My mother brought it back from Italy when I was around five. She told me that whenever she was away, I should look at the train and know that though it might take a while, she would always return. Why is it that those touching things parents say can only make you feel better temporarily? She always returned, yes, but where is she now?

Tile sits on the end of my bed and says quietly, "Why are you and Dad acting weird?"

"Tile, I need to go to sleep now. And so do you, it's way past your bedtime."

"I know. But I miss her."

He lays his head down near my leg.

"Come here," I say.

He comes closer and I hold him, trying my best to transfer any strength I may have left. He doesn't deserve to know what I know, not yet. He's just a kid.

After a minute he gets up and walks over to the night-light. He smooths his hands over it before pulling it out of its socket, making the room go completely dark.

CHAPTER 18

STAKEOUT

I call Oliver in the morning, and he says to come over at ten. His housekeeper answers the door, and this time she has a toddler with her, a boy with big bottle-brown eyes. I smile at him and he holds out his arms, so I pick him up. The housekeeper rolls her eyes as if to say, *Why don't you try being his mother for a while.* After a minute he gets squirmy. I let him down and he runs into the kitchen.

"I'm sorry, I never got your name."

"Denise," she says, pointing toward the kitchen. "And the little terror is Felipe. Oliver's in his room."

On my way up the stairs I look at the pictures that line the walls, all in clean silver frames. They are mostly of his parents at black-tie events, and a few of his mom on a horse. I wonder where his father is. The last I remember seeing him was a couple years ago—he always looked very serious.

When I get to his room, Oliver quickly hides the comic book that he's reading. I wonder if it's X-rated.

"Hey, Fifteen," he says, moving some curls out of his eyes.

"Hi. I met Felipe. He's adorable."

"Yeah, isn't he? He only comes when my mom's not here. It's our secret. The poor lady has to take care of him and he's not even her child. Her sister's a drug addict."

"Wow."

"Don't tell my mom."

"Of course not."

"So, what wild shenanigans are we partaking in today?"

I pull out my mother's phone.

"Well, my father confirmed she was having an affair with Cole, but he didn't say much more."

"Oh." He gives me a look of sympathy I try to eradicate by quickly introducing the next task. I jump up next to him on the bed.

"So, I want to check him out."

"Do you know where he lives?"

I scroll through my mom's contacts.

"No, but here's his number."

Oliver takes the phone and, to my surprise, immediately presses Call.

"Wait!"

He holds up his hand in an attempt to calm me down. Then he speaks slowly, in a deeper voice, and I am completely amazed at how authentic his impersonation sounds.

"Yes, I'm calling from DHL Express—I have a package to deliver but it seems we have the wrong address, could you confirm . . . yes . . . okay, great . . . yes, thank you, goodbye now."

I get off the bed and jump up and down a little. How easy was that? Even though I'm totally impressed, I try to tone it down and act normal. "Good thinking."

"I watch too many detective shows," he says.

The address is near the Laugh Lounge, and this time Oliver's driver takes us there. It's clear that the two of them have a "don't ask, don't tell" policy.

"Another secret?" the driver asks.

"You could say that," Oliver says.

As we race past the fancy doctors' offices on Park Avenue, I'm suddenly grateful that all this is happening, because it clearly has brought us closer. I try to imagine what it will feel like when he finally kisses me. Or maybe I will kiss him. Either way, I can tell it's coming, like someone standing behind me whose presence I can sense without looking back. I just have to turn at the right time.

Cole's apartment building is brand-new, sandwiched between two really old one-story brick buildings. It's a classic sign of gentrification, the new world overtaking the old. Yuppies replacing immigrants, getting elbow room by pushing out the locals. We stand outside and look up at the towering glass, then at each other.

"What now?" I ask.

Just then, a man with large black sunglasses and a trench coat pushes number twelve, Cole's apartment. Without saying a word, he gets buzzed in. I realize there's a security camera, so I grab Oliver and scoot us off to one side. A few minutes later the man comes back out empty-handed. We walk to the deli and get Cokes, then come back and see another person buzz, this time a girl, maybe eighteen, in a tracksuit. There is a man selling hats on the curb, and we pretend we're customers. Oliver puts a few on my head and smiles his approval. I almost forget that we are on a stakeout.

We move to the stairs across the street, which are flanked by a magnolia tree and some garbage bins. I decide to ask him about his dad.

He looks at me like, *Are we really getting into this?* I nod.

"He lives in Easthampton," he says, as if Easthampton is in Russia. His face goes tight and blank. I don't pry further. A toddler goes by carrying a mask and a snorkel.

"Oh, I just realized, we should go swimming sometime at Janine's building, there's this crazy pool."

Oliver's face goes very still, and he seems to be having a seizure of some kind. I get a little scared and ask him what's wrong.

"I don't swim," he says. He puts down his Coke carefully on the stoop.

"Oh." I'm not sure if I know him well enough to push further, but as if sensing my thoughts, he begins to explain, in a voice that I have to move a little closer to hear.

"My father . . . well, he's sort of like one of those annoying life-coach people. He feels like he has to . . . exercise control over everyone."

I watch his face and see a vulnerability I've never seen, like he might just crumble and start to cry like a baby. Instead, he stares at me hard, daring himself not to.

"I was around five, I think, maybe six. It was a pool party at a country club in Greenwich. I was the one geeky kid not swimming. And my father told me I had to get in the water. He had this look, like Harrison Ford or something. Like there was no way I was going to get out of it. So he ended up basically throwing me into the pool."

I laugh a little and then totally regret it. It's obvious he hasn't told anyone this before. I touch his shoulder in a gesture of apology.

"All I remember is, well, fearing for my life." Now he laughs, but it is one of those laughs that should've been a cry, or something else. "I just sunk down, until this lifeguard girl got me up onto the stairs. I thought I was going to die." He makes the non-laugh sound again. "My dad stormed off and I just sat there, coughing up water while the lifeguard held me in a tight embrace."

I can feel my eyes watering and Oliver smiles. A genuine smile, like maybe he's happy to have spoken about it.

"The weird thing is, I remember feeling so comforted, so safe in the arms of a complete stranger, this lifeguard. I wanted to go home with her, maybe have a different life."

I can't think of anything to say except "Wow," which makes me sound like a surfer. I sip the last of my Coke, which is now warm.

"When I got home after, there was a cello on my bed. My mother had bought it for me without telling my father. She had heard about what happened."

The sky is getting darker and it starts to mist a little. I don't think about getting wet, or my clothes, or my hair frizzing out. I just want to stay right where I am.

"Ever since then, music was the only thing I could escape into. Sometimes, when I see people out in the world with sad, hard expressions, I just want to reach out and put headphones on them, you know?"

I have felt the exact same way, and feel the urge to yell, *Yes!* But instead I simply smile and nod. We sit for a while just watching people walk by. It starts to rain a little more. He looks up at the sky.

"What's your *Singin' in the Rain*?"

I give him a puzzled look and he explains that his grandmother on his mother's side was his favorite person. She was a dancer and had three husbands. When she was dying, Oliver read to her for the last few weeks of her life. He didn't know what the book meant but tried his best to read it well, like he knew the story and was telling it off the top of his head. It's wonderful to see his eyes light up talking about her, but I still don't understand what it has to do with *Singin' in the Rain*.

"It was her favorite movie, and she said everyone had one, the movie that made you look at life differently."

Immediately, the answer comes to me. "*Witness.*"

He smiles. "Harrison Ford."

"Yes. Did you know he got his first movie part at age thirty-one?"

"That's a lot of tables to wait on. Why *Witness*?"

"It's definitely dark, but it's also beautifully shot. And I have this obsession with the Amish. They are from another world. I went on a shoot with my father in Pennsylvania and met a whole family of them. I gave this girl my old iPod and she had to hide it from her parents."

"Don't tell me you milked the cows."

"Ew, no!"

After a few more minutes, Cole comes out, lights a cigarette, and hops down the stairs. My mother hated cigarettes. One time she found some in my jacket and got really mad. They were Janine's but I didn't bother telling her that, as it seemed like such an obvious lie. She never would have stood for it with Cole. Maybe he recently took them up. He looks older than he does in the picture, and he seems a little more crouched, less confident.

Oliver nudges me and we whisper, even though he's across the street.

"I'm not exactly sure what I'm supposed to say to him."

"Well," Oliver says, "if you want to get to the bottom of what happened to your mother, I would advise befriending him first."

I start to get up just as Cole goes back inside. I run to

the curb but a stretch limo goes by, and by the time it passes Cole has shut the door.

I return to Oliver and sit down, defeated. He looks at me and says, "You're cute when you're mad."

The edges of our thighs touch, and I am hyperaware of it, as if there is a field of electric heat between us.

Nothing happens for a long time, except the two of us being together. So often people talk to fill the space between them, even if it's about the weather or simply to hear their own voices echo into the world. Oliver and I just sit in silence, observing the city life together, and it feels right.

"I guess this stakeout came up short," he says. The wind picks up and for a minute everything looks shadowed. With hardly any warning, thunder rips through the sky, giving way to a strong, diagonal rain. The building has only a tiny canopy so we are forced to stand really close. I have to remind myself that I'm not in one of my father's movies. We are laughing at the rain, even though it's not really funny. After our laughter settles, he reaches out and cups my chin again, and I know it's going to happen. Those lips that were alive only in my thoughts are now very alive in real life, closing in, slowly, until they reach mine and we both close our eyes.

CHAPTER 19

ON THE MARKET

Now that Oliver has kissed me, I am untouchable. At school I look the Rachels right in the eye and don't flinch. I cannot tell you how good this feels. How silly of me to even care about being friends with them. Janine and I sit down at our table across from the Rachels, who are eating yogurt and those little plastic cups filled with mandarin orange slices. We are having chicken tenders. When my mother died, the only thing that made me feel alive was eating. People assumed I wouldn't have an appetite, but I actually ate a lot. It was almost like my body became depleted by the loss and I had to eat more than normal to replenish it. So many people use food as a substitute for unfulfilled longing, but for me it was a necessity. Every girl at this table will probably stress about food and weight when we're older, but why do it now?

Our metabolism is crazy high, most of us are like Energizer Bunnies, so what's the point in getting all weird about food? The Rachels barely even finish their yogurt.

Since I know Janine has experience with boys, I decide to get some advice from her after lunch as we wait for assembly.

"Why do you ask? You still crushing on that neighbor of yours?"

"Yes. We kissed yesterday! He's supercute."

"Good for you, girl. Just stay away from hot dogs."

I smile. That's one of the cool things about Janine. She's smart enough to know that she made a mistake and should just move on. Being able to laugh at yourself is half the battle. Surprisingly, she tells me to take it slow with Oliver, make sure it's "organic."

There are girls at my school who wear these silly bracelets and preach about abstinence. There's something about them that creeps me out. Even our Health Ed teacher tells us that it's our own choice, that whatever we choose to do sexually, we just have to make sure we're safe and responsible. Aside from them, most everyone has experimented in my grade. I know I'm not superadvanced when it comes to the subject, but I'm not a total prude or anything. I just got sidetracked and kind of gypped out of last year because of Mom dying.

The assembly starts. It's a group of African dancers and percussionists. Their costumes are bright and beautiful, and their movements are raw and uninhibited. This does nothing to distract me from the subject of Oliver. He has such a gentle way about him. He makes all this affair-and-message business somehow worthwhile. I need to find out more about the night Mom died, and Cole is the missing link. I don't know what I'm going to find, but I'm so glad Oliver will be there with me.

The dancers join in a circle holding hands, then release them up into the air, creating what looks like a blooming flower. I realize that Mom is someone I would have talked to about Oliver. She wasn't really a typical mom. She was more like a friend. She never imposed her morals on me; she just encouraged me to create my own ways of thinking and dealing with things. Talking with her always made me feel better, no matter the subject. We would fight, of course, but not that often. Most of the time she was like a sounding board, and though Janine is not a bad substitute, I feel my mother's absence sharply once again. I sigh discreetly. *Will this feeling ever go away?*

On the way home from school I stop by her studio. The cleaning woman is there again; she motions toward her supplies but I say, "No, *gracias.*"

When I get inside, I open her laptop and see the picture again. I was wearing a purple sweatshirt that I don't even remember owning. I think it was borrowed. We rented a house every year in Nantucket, and sometimes the other families would leave stuff behind that would become ours. I wonder where the owner of that sweatshirt is now.

I close my eyes and tell myself to just do it. I open up

the file that says "Luna," and there's a date in the corner, about a month before she died. It's written in diary format. There are only three entries. I start to read the first one:

> When we brought you home from the hospital, your father was terrified something was going to happen to you. For the first three nights, when you weren't nursing, he sang to you and tried to tell you jokes. He canceled one of his biggest movie deals ever to stay home with you. I had to force him to go out, get some air, making up things I needed so he could leave us alone. He was so caring, so genuine, that I told myself then and there I would never leave him. Now, over a decade later, so much has changed. . . .

My mother was pretty open with me, but how much do we really see of the people we love? The fact that she wrote this, to me but in private, is strange—almost like she knew she was going to die.

I pause and look out at the darkening sky, thinking of my dad, whose nurturing I could have used later in my life, when his attention was always somewhere else. When I turned four my mother threw me a birthday party, and it was mostly adults. She was very pregnant with Tile, and my father couldn't come for some reason or another. I know I was superyoung but I remember being sad, because I never related to my "friends" at the time. When you're four, kids just come to your birthday party for the food, and the parents pick out all the presents anyway. My mother seemed almost *happy* that my father couldn't make it. She was in her last trimester and drinking a glass of champagne. I blew out the candles on the cake and felt empty inside.

> . . . your father is the same man, but I fear I am not the same woman. When we met, as you know, I couldn't really be bothered. But he did all the right things. He made me feel more special than any photographer or camera or fashion spread ever has. I was finally the center of someone's universe. But that was quixotic. It was simply something that swept me up . . .

I wonder if she's talking about the same thing I'm experiencing with Oliver. There's a feeling I get with him that almost hurts, a small ache in the bottom of my stomach, but at the same time I crave it. Maybe that's what the cutters are about, or Janine's dad, who she once caught getting whipped by a woman who looked like Halle Berry in *Batman*. I never understood the appeal of pain, but now I'm starting to.

> . . . and now it's spitting me out. Something is changing beyond my control, like gravity. I am falling faster every day. There is someone I have been connected to for a long, long time. He challenges me to think outside the lines I so rigidly drew for myself. He loves me, yes. He wants me, yes. He wants to make me happy. He gets pleasure

from it. Your father made me happy for a long time,
but I'm not sure that any one person can make
another person happy forever. Humans are living
things, and the deeper our roots go, the more
complex the flower. I am not sure your father even
recognizes who I have become. . . .

I'm not sure I'm recognizing her, either. My mother was
intelligent and sharp-tongued, and there's something in
her writing that seems soft around the edges. I realize that
my palms are sweating. I wash my hands in her tiny sink,
go to the refrigerator, and pour myself a glass of water. I
don't drink it, I just let it sit there, and continue to read.

. . . It's not his fault, it's not anyone's fault. Oh,
Luna, I hope I am making sense. You see, he thinks
I'm having an affair. I'm not, officially. But I do feel
myself slipping. I know you're probably too young
to hear any of this, which is why I am typing it
instead of telling you. Most of my friends would
think I'm a nut job, and the ones who would like to
hear it would probably just spread the word. All the
people in my life, except Richard, would either
judge me or just gossip about it. . . .

I start to cry a little. *Where are you now, Mom? Why
couldn't you have come shopping with me for a bra? Why do
I have to get advice from Janine?* I feel so angry I could
throw her laptop through the window. I gulp the Pellegrino and suddenly hear a key turn in the lock. My heart
leaps through my chest as I close the laptop and pour the
rest of my Pellegrino into one of the dead plants.

"Oh, well, hello there," says a woman who's trying way too hard with her outfit. Behind her is a young couple, dressed in Gap, with soft, eager faces.

"Oh, hi, I didn't realize . . ."

"You must be Jules's daughter."

"Yes, hi."

"Kit Langley, with Citi Habitats. Your father put the property on the market yesterday. Shall we give you a minute?"

"No, it's okay. I was just leaving anyway."

I realize there are still tears on my face. I grab my bag and walk past them, trying to smile and be normal.

From the third-floor landing I can hear Kit using her key words. *Cozy. Light-drenched.* I have to talk to my father about this. Why didn't he consult me? Was he afraid of the things I'd find if I went back there? It's too late for that.

The streets are piled with trash bags stacked in front of the pristine brownstones. Some window cleaners whistle at me, and I realize for the first time that though they definitely aren't as big as Janine's, I have noticeable breasts. With my hair down I could probably pass for eighteen. When I get back home I go right into my father's office.

"You're selling Mom's place?"

"Moon, it's empty. I should have sold it months ago. What do you want me to do?"

"I want to use it after school, to do my homework and stuff."

He looks at me, knowing I have more leverage now. The

more information I find out about him, the more transparent he becomes. I am chipping away at his exterior.

"The maintenance is over a thousand a month, my accountant—"

"Screw the accountant. I'm not ready for you to just sell Mom's place like it's some . . . investment."

I don't really know what I'm saying, but I'm furious. At my mom for leaving the world, at my dad for lying to me, at the Rachels for thinking they're so cool, and at myself for not being smart enough to see it all coming.

His phone rings. It says *Birnbaum, Alex*—his agent.

"I have to take this."

"Good," I say, turning to leave, "you'll be needing more jobs to pay the maintenance."

He widens his eyes at me and I smile like I'm kidding, but I'm really not.

CHAPTER 20

PARTNERS IN CRIME?

I find a note taped to my door when I get home:

> *fifteen—*
> *5:30—my roof—6th floor*
> *be there—*
>
> *o*

I look at my watch: 5:28. I drop my bag and turn right around, tucking the note into my back pocket. When I get to the sixth floor and open the exit door, Oliver greets me with a bowl of popcorn and points to the recliner chairs set up in the center of the roof.

"How'd you get those up here?"

"I know people."

I smile, walk slowly over to them, and sit down. I guess our second try at talking to Cole will have to wait.

He says, "Stay right here."

I hear the hum of a projector and see a large white square of light appear on the side of the next building, and then the first shot: golden fields and blue sky. It's my favorite movie!

"*Witness*," he says. "Your *Singin' in the Rain*."

I feel like the luckiest girl on the Upper West Side.

During the movie, Oliver refills my Sprite and occasionally holds my hand.

"How the hell did you do this?" I ask him.

"Isaac, the guy in the penthouse. He shows movies up here sometimes. I tutor his son in math, so I pulled a string."

"Wow." There I go again. Surfer talk.

As always, the movie is riveting and very human. I'm so happy that I don't even mind Oliver falling asleep a little toward the end. When the credits roll I catch him looking at me with that incredible smile. I blush a little and turn toward him, waiting for the inevitable, and there it is again: his violet lips, soft as a cloud, and everything becomes irrelevant. I am drowning in a moment I hope will never end.

The next day Oliver meets me at the Creperie. I thank him profusely for the movie and he waves it away like it was nothing. He gets a call from his father, I can tell by his voice. He becomes very tense, and it's strange watching the transformation. When he hangs up I say, "Gosh, he must really have some claws on you."

"You don't even know. He calls me like three times a day. He knows my routine has changed since I met you, and he's not happy about it."

I feel my heart sink a little.

"He doesn't want you to have a life?"

"Not really. He's only concerned with my cello and my schoolwork. He's like, you can have fun later. It's weird, though, because he doesn't even live with me and it's like a shadow following me. He's really strict, like his father was with him."

We get ginger ales and *pommes frites*, and again, he orders in perfect French.

"We have to talk to this Cole character," I tell him.

"Are you sure you're ready for this?"

"How much worse can it get?"

He looks at me and smiles, and for a second everything goes away, like the kiss on the roof. My face is probably the color of a ripe tomato. I feel like I am what love songs are made of.

On the way downtown, Oliver holds my hand on the subway. I secretly wish the Rachels could see me now. The train lights go off for a minute and Oliver kisses me again, and I hear myself moan with pleasure. I remember Rachel One bringing a porno DVD she had stolen from her brother into school and we watched some of it on her laptop. There was an Asian girl on top of a chubby white guy, and she was almost singing, obviously faking it. I feel like I could do that right now, and wonder if the Asian girl wasn't. I look at Oliver after the lights go back on. He's probably never seen a porno. Suddenly I want him to be mine to corrupt, forever.

We stake out Cole's apartment again from across the street. A drag queen walks by looking like he/she just got into a fight. She asks us for a cigarette.

"Do we look like we smoke?" Oliver says.

She makes a sound with her lips and walks off in a huff.

"I think she likes you," I tease.

"Yeah? I've always had a soft spot for transvestites."

We share a Snapple and a chocolate bar. I almost feel like it's another date, like we're not waiting for my mother's secret lover to exit his building.

"Can you imagine feeling like you're the wrong gender?" I ask.

"I had this teacher in fifth grade, Mr. Jagel. One Halloween he came to school dressed as a girl. Everyone called him Fag-el after that. The thing is, I really liked him. He wasn't gay, he was just open-minded. And a little silly."

"My mom had so many gay friends. Everyone she worked with. The makeup people, the photographers, even her literary agent."

"You mean her gay-gent?"

I laugh. Oliver's eyes are pools of warmth, and his hair is so perfect I could cry.

"My father has a gay-gent too," I add.

Oliver smiles. "I remember visiting my cousins who live in Utah. We went to this ski camp and there was this one kid who wore his scarf the French way, you know? And they kept calling him a fag and stuff, and I told them to stop, said that I was gay too just to teach them a lesson."

"Good for you."

"Besides, the scarf looked kind of cool."

"Well, I'm glad we're not ignorant country bumpkins."

"What exactly is a bumpkin, anyway?"

He looks at me and we both break out into laughter. The moment is quickly squashed by the sound of the large door opening across the street and Cole emerging. I throw away our Snapple and the candy wrapper and we follow him west. He ducks into a coffee shop and we stand outside at a loss.

"Okay, Fifteen, we've got to do something."

"When he comes out, ask him for directions."

Oliver nods, as if that's a good plan.

Cole comes back out wearing huge aviator glasses and carrying a large coffee.

"Excuse me," Oliver says, "do you know where the A train is?"

He stops, gives us a funny look, and says, "You're on the wrong side of town, I'm afraid."

After an uncomfortable moment, I say, "It's fine, Cole, we'll figure it out."

Oliver looks at me hard.

"What?" Cole says. "How do you know my name?"

"Listen," Oliver says, "do you have a minute?"

Cole runs his free hand through his hair and nods. I notice that he has very blue eyes. "I could spare a couple."

Back inside the coffee shop, a bunch of people are crouched over their laptop screens, and it smells like cinnamon. The sun has overwarmed the place, so I take off my sweater. We sit down at a corner table.

"This is Luna," Oliver says, "and from what we understand you were close with her mother."

When Cole realizes who I am, he looks at the floor, then out the window, then at his fingernails—anywhere but into my eyes. Oliver excuses himself to go to the bathroom and I start to talk softly.

"Look, I just want to know what happened. Were you with her at Butter the night she died?"

"Yes." He finally looks me in the eyes. "I can't believe how much you've grown. I met you once but you were . . . little."

I plop the cuff links down on the table.

"Are these yours?"

Now he looks a little scared. He picks up the cuff links and turns them around in his cupped hand as if they dropped from the sky.

"Were you there when she got hit by the cab?"

He looks at me again, his bright eyes burning into mine.

"How did you find me?"

"What does it matter?"

He sips his coffee and his phone rings. He hits mute

and puts it in his pocket. I try to see what my mother saw in him. He's attractive, but maybe he's like a smooth stone that when turned over reveals darkness underneath. Oliver comes back and sits close, fortifying me.

"Look, it was no one's fault. Your dad, he was very distraught."

"Duh," Oliver says.

"Listen, are you two allowed to be . . ."

"No, we're skipping kindergarten," I say.

His phone buzzes again.

"Luna, listen . . . your mother was a . . . friend of mine. I am so sorry about what happened."

"Just a friend?" Oliver is skeptical.

"It's complicated," he says. "I'd be happy to talk to you about this further but I have a meeting." He stands up, bows slightly, then leaves in a daze.

Oliver and I don't say anything for a while. Cole has left us calculating in silence. Oliver's phone rings again and I see it's his father. He makes a grunting noise and answers it. He walks to the corner and I can tell he is very frustrated. When he finishes the call, he looks up at the ceiling for a minute, as if praying.

On the way uptown our subway car is empty. I rest my head on Oliver's shoulder and he brushes his fingers along the underside of my wrist. I listen to the rumble and try to let it drown out the thoughts in my head.

The last time I saw my mother was the day I left for camp. I came into her room and she and my father were sitting on opposite sides of the bed, facing away from each other. She turned and motioned me toward her, hugged me a little too desperately.

"Make sure you keep in touch while you're up there," she said with damp eyes. She was wearing a wispy red scarf tied loosely around her neck. I wasn't sure if her fragile state was because I was leaving, or if something had happened before I walked into the room. Had they been talking about Cole? Then my father abruptly stood up and said, "Let's get this show on the road." It was not the sort of thing he would say, and even though I could sense something was wrong, I was too wrapped up in my own world: the anticipation of camp, who my counselor was going to be, which kids were going to return, whether I had packed everything I needed. Now, as the train continues to barrel through the dark underground, I wonder how I could've been so immune to those moments, those signs that I can only see now, after it has all happened, after she's gone. For the most part they were happy, and I guess I bought into all the good stuff so much that I was in denial about what was underneath. It's like that line Richard quotes about Mrs. Dalloway, "Always throwing parties to cover the silence." My parents did entertain a lot, and that is when you put on your game face. I am just so curious now. When did the façade start to crumble?

* * *

I take Oliver to my mother's studio and he walks around it carefully, as if it's a crime scene. He sits on the windowsill and says, "Aren't you going to read more of what she wrote?"

"Yes, but not today. I usually hate this word, especially 'cause my counselor at school uses it so much, but I still have to *process* everything."

Oliver walks up to me, puts two hands on my shoulders, then pulls me into an embrace. Part of me wants to let go of everything, lose myself in his skin, his silky curls, the pools of his eyes. Instead I just let him hold me.

Suddenly I realize that I'm starving. As if hearing my thoughts, Oliver says, "Well, could you process a pizza?" I smile and nod.

We sit at a table in the front of Ray's Pizza—the original one, yeah right—and eat steaming slices. There are hundreds of "Ray's Famous" pizza places and every one claims to be the original. Either way, it's yummy. I get cheese and Oliver gets pepperoni. At first, we are ravenous, and then we both pause to take a break.

"Are you thinking what I'm thinking?" he asks.

"What he said about my father being distraught?"

"Yes. I hate to say this, Fifteen, but I feel like there's still something he's not telling you."

"I know."

We finish our pizza and walk home. On the way he gets another call from his father, and at one point he tells me to hold on and goes into an alley for privacy. I can hear his voice rising and it kind of scares me. The gentle boy has angst. Why is his father so hard on him? He comes back to join me looking really pale, like he just found out someone died.

"Is everything okay?"

"Not really," he says, "not at all."

While we walk I try not to press him, just let him have his space. He doesn't hold my hand and I can feel the absence. All of a sudden I feel terribly alone.

When we get to my stoop, a look comes over his face I have never seen before. The only way I can describe it is cold.

"I have a recital coming up, it's a preliminary thing for the Paris show. I have to learn a bunch of new pieces."

I feel like I'm standing on a small rock in the middle of the ocean and he's getting on a boat, waving goodbye. He looks like a totally different person. The eyes that covered me with warmth have now gone somewhere else, looking through me.

"Cool," I say, trying to sound nonchalant even though my whole body is practically shaking, its core the epicenter of an impending earthquake. "Thanks for, you know, everything."

"I may not be that, well, available for a while."

That's fine, I'll just stand here until the water rises and I drown.

"Okay, I understand."

And that's it. He just turns around. No kiss, no touch, no smile. I watch him walk into his house and I stand there for what seems like an hour, until I hear Tile yell down from the window. I look up and see him, waving his hands up in the air, wondering what the heck I'm doing, oblivious to the fact that I may have lost the only boy I've ever loved.

CHAPTER 21

INNOCENCE

For the first time ever, I keep Tile out of my room. All I want to do is crawl under a rock and stay there for a year. I know that Oliver's dad really stresses him out, but I didn't think the guy ran his life. I think about calling Janine, but decide against it. I busy myself with mindless math homework until I hear the familiar bling of an IM on my computer.

> **Dariaposes:** Hey girl how is Cello boy?
> **Moongirlnyc:** Long story—not sure
> **Dariaposes:** Did you kiss him?

I blush at the thought of it.

> **Moongirlnyc:** Yes
> **Dariaposes:** Then he'll be back

Moongirlnyc: ☺ Hope so
Dariaposes: Listen, I'm working on a show for your photographs—but it's still a maybe, no green light yet
Moongirlnyc: What?
Dariaposes: I took them to my friend who has a gallery in Williamsburg

I start to type but I can't find words. A *show?*

Moongirlnyc: Omg
Dariaposes: But need more shots, like maybe 10
Moongirlnyc: Sure! I was actually going to bring my cam to school
Dariaposes: Good
Moongirlnyc: When would it be?
Dariaposes: Not sure. Does your dad mind us mentioning you're his daughter?

I freeze. *Please don't let this be about him.* So many times in my life—too many to count—people showed interest in me because they wanted to get to him. I decide to be vague.

Moongirlnyc: Not sure
Dariaposes: Doesn't really matter. But your age will help a lot
Moongirlnyc: Why?
Dariaposes: For press . . . they eat up young talent

Even though she makes it sound like I'm a cupcake, I'm very intrigued by the idea. Maybe Ms. Gray was right, this could be my calling.

Moongirlnyc: Whatever you say
Dariaposes: Work on more shots, and keep it raw
Moongirlnyc: Ok
Dariaposes: You're going to be a star miss Luna
Moongirlnyc: We'll see about that
Dariaposes: And all the cello boys will be lining up

I blush again, and there's a knock at my door.

Moongirlnyc: Gotta go, ttys
Dariaposes: Ciao4now

It's Tile again. This time I let him in. He walks over to my bed, plops himself down, and says, "She's here again. Mushroom lady."

"What?"

"I figured it out. She smells like mushrooms."

"Well, it could be worse."

"So what did Dad tell you?"

I close my laptop, turn to him, and sigh. He's not going to let up.

"He just told me she was spending time with someone named Cole." I walk over and sit down next to him, grab the racquetball he is squeezing out of his hand. "Tile, it doesn't matter now. Like you said, she's dead."

He looks at me hard. "Dead as a doornail," he says.

I give him back the ball and he starts bouncing it on the floor. I don't want to tell him I've met Cole, that she was seeing him, and that there's something still missing about the night she died. The articles in Page Six and *US*

Weekly on her "tragic death" simply reported that she had been with "a friend." I had always assumed it was her yoga teacher, like Dad told me. Now I know it was Cole, and I'm afraid of what I might find out, afraid that the information might somehow scar me more than I already am. But it's too late. It's like scratching a scab, and the blood has already started to trickle.

Tile is concentrating on the ball, and looks so innocent, so unscarred. He doesn't have his mother, but it hasn't really sunk in for him. He has dealt with it in a very literal and unemotional way. I feel a crushing in my heart knowing that soon enough, he will really feel the weight of what happened and will have to carry it with him like I do, the heaviness of loss.

"You know all those videos you took of Mom when Dad gave you the Flip video camera last year?"

"Yeah, most of them are boring."

"Well, I tell you what, why don't you upload them into my computer and I'll make a little short film, to memorialize her."

His eyes light up and he stops bouncing the ball. "Can I choose the sound track?"

I smile, thinking that Blink-182 is not exactly what I had in mind.

"Sure."

He runs out to get his Flip video and returns in seconds. After we upload them, I tell him I need private time. He nods, but then walks up to me, cowering a little.

He looks me in the eye and I turn away. It's heartbreaking, how much I want to keep him safe from the world, and how hopeless a notion that is.

"You know, maybe sometime you can have Oliver over. We can play Xbox. Even though I can go to level six on Tomb Raider I can let him win."

I try to will my eyes not to water.

"Okay, Tile, sounds good."

Before he shuts the door, he turns around and says, "On second thought, you can pick the sound track. But I want my name in the credits."

CHAPTER 22

SHOW-AND-TELL

Before I hear the next message I decide to just concentrate on taking some decent pictures. The next day I bring my vintage camera to school, and people look at me strangely as I lug it through the hallway. The first thing I do is set it up in the girls' bathroom. There are two barred windows above the sink where washed-out morning light bleeds in. When the Rachels come in for their pre-homeroom touch-up, even Rachel Two says the words "Hey, you." I quickly realize that it's merely because there's a camera in the room. The first picture I take is the two Rachels from behind, standing underneath the window. Rachel One is admiring herself and Rachel Two is bent over to fix her tights. There are random objects on the sink, and the mirror is partly clouded up. I remember my father telling me that film is all about reflection. I wonder if this can be true with photography. I shoot.

Rachel One looks at me like she's hurt.

"You never called me."

"Sorry," I say, "I've been busy."

They look at each other and roll their eyes, and my stomach turns. Somehow nothing I say or do will make them grow up, or understand that this is not an episode of *Gossip Girl* or a chapter in *The Clique*.

The second picture I take is at lunch, outside in the quad. Jared, the ninth-grade stoner, has drawn a huge city on the sidewalk in chalk. It is beautifully intricate. I shoot it lengthwise, with his arm in the edge of the frame, about thirty thin black leather bracelets on his wrist, his hand almost completely white from the chalk.

I get to English early to show Ms. Gray the camera, and not surprisingly she bubbles over with excitement. I decide that if I ever take a picture of someone's face—a portrait—it will be hers. She stands right in front of the lens, and the only way I can describe her is honest. Nothing to hide. She looks like she wants to save the world, then make you dinner. I tell her she's a natural.

After I show the camera to the class and everyone gets a chance to look through the lens, Ms. Gray asks me if I'd like to take a picture. I say yes, but I have a specific request.

"As long as we keep our clothes on," she says. A few kids laugh.

"If everyone could put their feet up on the desks, just for a minute."

Ms. Gray looks apprehensive, but then nods, as if it's now the class assignment. For a few moments, I feel like my father directing a scene. I have a few kids cross ankles, and arrange some shoes so that they look askew. Then I tell everyone to freeze. I take the shot and it looks cool: the soles of everyone's shoes resting on top of the desks at all different angles, with a giant map of the world in the background.

I leave the camera in English for the rest of my classes, then retrieve it at the end of the day. As I pack it up, Ms. Gray says, "How is everything at home?"

I sit on the edge of her desk.

"Fine. My dad's seeing someone."

"Really?" Ms. Gray tries to play it down but I can tell by her face that her mind's working fast.

"She's an English teacher."

"Can't say I disapprove. Is it weird for you?"

I finish packing up the camera and don't answer.

"Dumb question," she says. "What about Tile?"

"He's ten, you know? I think it hasn't really sunk in."

"Yes, well, when it does, he'll be glad to have someone like you as a sister."

I know that Ms. Gray isn't saying that just to be nice, that she means it. She knows who I am, that deep down I have good intentions. This makes me feel, for a brief moment as I turn to leave, hopeful.

On the way home, however, I begin my descent into reality. Why did Oliver turn so cold yesterday? What did Cole mean about my father being distraught?

I tell my driver to take my camera home and drop me off at the studio. I feel it's time to continue reading the Luna file.

Inside, something seems different, the furniture moved slightly. I carefully sit down at her laptop and grab the phone. There's one message left, but I'm afraid of what it might be, that it will be a hang-up or something that isn't a payoff of some kind. I decide to wait. I double-click the file and continue where I had left off.

> . . . his films, those are his real loves. And you, Luna. He loves you more than anything and always has. When I told him about what was going on, his first concern was you—not himself, not Tile—you. He wanted to make sure you never knew, he thought it would destroy you. But I think his expectations for himself are so high, he wants to be perfect in your eyes. You are old enough to know that no one is perfect, right? The world I have been living in, the so-called glamour that you will read about in my book someday, is far from perfect. But how could I have known that I would meet the love of my life at the wrong time? And should I let him pass me by?

I read the words again and think of Oliver. *Love of my life.* How can she write that? I think of Cole in the coffee shop, so different from Dad, so easily readable. Nervous, exposed . . . scared, even. I can't remember my father ever being scared, or at least giving away that he was. Although my instinct is to hate Cole, I don't. There was something else in his eyes—remorse, compassion.

On our wedding day, while I was getting ready, your uncle Richard asked me if I really knew what I was doing. I never answered, because I'm not sure we ever really know what we are doing. We feel things in our hearts, make decisions, hear voices in our heads that tell us what to do, but in the end we never know how things will turn out. In all honesty, I will never stop loving your father . . .

What? It's like I'm reading words written by another person entirely. My mother was so self-assured, so together, almost meticulous in her ways. In one of my earliest memories I was collecting shells on the beach in Nantucket, and lining them all up on an old wooden table in the rented house. I always liked to put things in perfect lines. After taking a bath, I came back to the table and one was missing. My mother said it was cracked, so she had thrown it away. Maybe that shell was symbolic, like a mirror held up to a deep part of herself she couldn't bear to face. She was the cracked shell.

. . . or you. But I don't know if I can stop what's happening to me. I feel like this person has swung open doors and let light into places I never knew existed. I feel like I'm floating. . . .

The scary thing is that I know what she's talking about, sort of. On the subway, when I was resting my head on Oliver's shoulder and parts of his hair tickled my forehead, the train might just as well have been a plane, something with wings. I felt suspended above everything: the city, time, the hard, cold edges of the world. It was fleeting, but it's a memory I can still feel.

CHAPTER 23

RED FLAGS

I remember I have a dentist appointment, so I make my way down to Sixty-Third Street. My former dentist, a funny and kind man, has been replaced by an Indian guy who's very soft-spoken and eternally sad. The receptionist, a college kid named Levi with obviously dyed black hair and a nose ring, is a photographer. He gave me and Tile a flyer for a show he did once. I never got to go, but I remember the image on the postcard. It was an arm reaching into white space, and in the distance was a reddish sky. Something about it resonated with me, so I taped it to my locker.

"Hey, he's running a little late," Levi says.

"Who, Mr. Sunshine?"

He smiles. "Rays and rays of it."

I tell him about my camera, shooting Daria, and the

possibility of a show. He mentions this cool blog that tons of photographers are on, and how he got picked for representation through it. It was what led to his own show.

"So receptionist is not the end goal?" I ask.

"Safe to say."

I sink down into the giant couch in the waiting room, and it seems to eat me alive. I can barely see the top of Levi's head as he answers the phones, which are very persistent. When I'm called in ten minutes later, I have to wrench myself out of the thing.

Mr. Smiley cleans my teeth as I watch Rachael Ray cook something that involves pork and mushrooms on the monitor above the dentist chair. When he's finished and I get up to leave, I think I see a hint of a grin, but then I realize he's burping.

I get home to Tile, Elise, and my father eating in the dining room again. At least it's not the stew. They are having takeout from Thai Palace, and I'm excruciatingly hungry. Instead of scolding me for being out late, Dad simply says, "Moon, we got you the yellow coconut curry."

"Thanks," I say, taking a seat.

Elise is looking at me with this overblown smile, like I'm five, and it's irritating. I have an urge to dunk her head into the steaming soup. As usual, Tile is smothering his chicken satay in peanut sauce.

"So, Moon, what did you do today?"

Somehow I think *Read Mom's diary* wouldn't be appropriate, so I concentrate on the other stuff. "I took my camera to school, got some good shots."

"Tiley says you also shot a model by the park?"

I look at Tile. He's pretending to concentrate on chewing the chicken and not returning my gaze. I haven't prepared an answer for how I know Daria. Nothing comes so I just look at Tile hard and say, "Yes."

That settles it. We eat in silence. The curry tastes good, and I remember how much of it I ate after Mom died. Almost every day for months. My mother didn't like Thai food; she preferred Japanese. Whenever we ate Thai, she would have her own little tray of sushi from Whole Foods. She was an expert at using the chopsticks. Sometimes she'd put unused ones in her hair. She never ate dessert, unless it was fruit. She was always conscious of her diet but not obsessive, like Rachel One's mother, who's so thin she looks sickly. She would discourage Rachel from eating carbs or sugar, even when we were ten! As I bite into a moist chunk of potato, I'm so thankful that my mother never imposed any phobias on me. Rachel One will probably always have issues with food, and it won't be pretty. So many girls and women suffer from eating disorders, and to me it seems so useless. Why spend so much energy on making yourself look like an airbrushed waif in a magazine? My mother was skinny, but she was strong. She did Pilates and yoga. There are so many challenges that the world brings, why waste all that worry on the shape of your body? There's nothing sadder than hearing the tenth graders at my school throwing up in the girls' room. *Try losing your mother,* I often think. *That will give you something to throw up about.*

Elise attempts to clear my plate but I say, "It's okay, I got it."

The plan is to go to the movies, but I opt to stay home. Dad asks me if everything's all right, even though he knows it's not. Why do adults insist on asking important questions at the wrong time? Why not just wait to ask me when it's the right time, when we can actually talk?

"I'm fine," I say, sick of white lies.

As they are leaving, Tile says, "Want me to bring you back Gummi Bears?"

I smile and shake my head.

After they leave, I go into my room and walk over to the window. I know Oliver is practicing, but the blinds are drawn. I see Tile's Flip camera still stuck into my computer, the files all uploaded. I start to watch the footage.

It's mostly terrible. Handheld is not even the word. More like earthquake. There's one great sequence, though, where my mother is steaming some wineglasses and wiping them with a small white towel. She's wearing a pale green dress, and her hair is unusually wispy. She looks so beautiful, so at ease. The steam makes her face flush a little and she laughs at the camera when Tile asks, "How long have you worked in this household?"

I save that section and try to find other bits I can use. There is a POV shot entering the master bedroom, and I can hear my mother say something out of the shot. In a screenplay this would be called OS, for *offstage*. It's a simple sentence, but knowing what I know now, it is rooted in a whole other story.

It's over, Jules.

I look at the date of the clip: three weeks before she died. What's over? A TV show? The marriage? The affair?

The camera sweeps quickly past my father, who looks, as Cole mentioned, "distraught." Then my mother comes into the frame and turns on the charm, spinning around, modeling her nightgown. How can she just switch gears like that if she was talking about what I think she was talking about?

Tile asks her how old she is.

"Twenty-nine," she jokes.

"And what's your favorite color?"

"Red. The color of passion."

She looks across the room, presumably at my father, and her face deflates a little.

Then the clip gets cut off.

The next few segments are too shaky, but there's one that is salvageable. She's getting ready to leave, putting a scarf and a jacket over her dress, and she does it effortlessly. The whole time, she's looking at the camera with an expression of truth. She is not trying to be glamorous, or funny, or pretty. She's just being herself. I pause it, and stare into her eyes.

Truth. If it really is our skin, why is it so hard to live by? All that time I witnessed my parents' life together, there was nothing I thought more "true." I remember noticing the way Rachel One's parents acted around each other, almost as if they were business partners—everything so rigid and planned, no affection, no longing in their eyes. I knew that wasn't "true." But in my house, seeing my mother throw her head back and do her angel laugh, my dad pinch her butt, kiss her lightly on the delicate skin below her ear . . . all of this was the truth. And now, crushing me with more weight than her being gone is the realization of that truth being an illusion, that their love wasn't strong enough to hold them together. If they built a love to withstand time, why did it crumble?

I walk to the window once more. The light is on now but the blinds are still drawn. I picture Oliver working on his pieces, his eyes closed in concentration, his soft hand caressing the bow.

I will not give up on you, Oliver. Sometimes the love we build is meant to survive.

CHAPTER 24

TREADING WATER

The next day after school I find myself at Rachel One's house. I was in a daze all day, just going through the motions, and when she asked me to come over, I just said yes without even thinking about it. Now, in her chocolate-brown-and-pink-trimmed room, with pictures of Zac Efron and Penn Badgley everywhere, I feel like I have to get to the bottom of something.

"Why do you want to be friends with me again?"

She brushes her golden locks, which she does so much it's a wonder they don't just fall off.

"It's not that we weren't friends, it's just, you sort of went off the deep end for a while."

"Isn't that when you need friends the most?"

"Babe, I tried. Remember? You told me I should go back into my Barbie box."

Did I say that? I hold back a smile.

"Fair enough. But I'm still skeptical."

"You've always been that way." She holds up her butterfly hair clips. "Now, what do you think, purple or blue?"

Like I care. Still, I humor her. "Blue, definitely. Matches your eyes."

"Okay, now tell me, who is it?"

"What?"

"You've been walking around school in a romantic haze. I'm no Einstein, but I know when someone is in love. C'mon, I want dish. Who is it?"

Is it that obvious? I feel myself blushing yet again. I suppose if there's anyone who's going to get it out of me, it's Rachel One.

"Well, he lives across the street from me. He plays the cello."

"Sounds McDreamy. Name?"

"Oliver."

She starts applying lip liner for what I assume to be the tenth time today. "Good name. Old money."

As if on cue, Rachel One's mother comes to the door, asking if we want a snack. She is so perfectly put-together she looks almost grotesque. When you try too hard, sometimes it has the opposite effect. It may be that she's had too much work done on her face.

"Sure," I say. Rachel looks at me like I'm crazy to even consider putting something in my mouth, let alone swallowing it.

"Which Hampton do they summer in?"

I have to laugh at this question coming from a fifteen-year-old, but I answer it nonetheless.

"His dad lives in Easthampton, but I think his parents are . . . separated."

"Hmm."

Rachel is now inspecting her pores and, at the same time it seems, devising a plan. Although I'm not opposed to beauty tips, that's about as far as I'll go in letting Rachel get involved in the Oliver situation.

Her mother comes back with rice cakes and dried apricots and places them on the desk, along with a bottle of Pellegrino, which never fails to remind me of my father. I'm going to have to talk to him once and for all, and get things completely out in the open.

When her mother leaves, Rachel turns away from the mirror and looks at me.

"How far have you gone?"

"We've only kissed. But he's so sweet. He helped me with . . . stuff. But the other day he totally changed. Like, his face turned cold and he said he had to work on his cello a lot for his upcoming recital."

"Fear of commitment."

"Rachel, it's not like we're getting married."

"Babe, it happens all the time. You were getting too close."

I am astonished to think that she may be right.

"Stay cool," she says. "Keep your distance. He'll come around."

That's what Daria said.

"Come on, let's go down to the theater."

I grab a rice cake on the way out and we head down to the movie theater, which is actually in her house. I spent many childhood afternoons dwarfed by its black walls and huge leather couches, watching Disney movies, oblivious to what the world had in store for me.

Before we get ten minutes into *Bring It On*, I realize it's time for me to hear the last message. One of the reasons why I have waited is that each message is getting me closer and closer to her death, and part of me knows that the last message is the last thing she would have heard, perhaps in the same hour she died, and it's all a little creepy. But something tells me the time is now.

I bring my bag into the floral-wallpapered bathroom with eighty-dollar candles lining the toilet, and look for my mom's phone. It's not there.

I'm not sure how long I remain in the bathroom before I hear Rachel One knocking. I flush the toilet, then open the door.

"You okay?" she asks. "You look a little pale."

I tell her I don't feel good and have to go. I run through all the places I've been, trying to think where I could've left it. The studio is where I last listened, but I remember having it after that at home.

Back in my room I go through everything, but no luck. *Do not tell me I have lost the phone before hearing the last message!* Especially if it contains the crucial detail, like something in a photograph that completes the picture.

To keep myself busy, I scan some of my images into my computer and check out the blog Levi mentioned. I notice there's a link to a contest for best city photograph. I decide I'll use the one with the kid drawing the city in chalk. It costs twenty dollars to submit a picture, so I'll use the credit card my dad gave me for emergencies. I know this isn't one, but I think I deserve it, considering. I look at some of the photographers' work and feel really, really humbled. How could I even dream of being in the same league as these people? But then I read a blog about how art is subjective and even untrained people can have a gift and just not know it. This gives me hope.

I take a break from the computer and try to concentrate on my math final. For some reason, I've always studied on my bed. It helps me to have the space to spread things around. I usually get back cramps but do it anyway. I start reviewing my geometry, which Janine hates but I'm pretty good at, even though it seems like stretching your brain for some workout it will never do in real life. When am I going to have to use the Pythagorean theorem?

Halfway through reviewing my first lesson plan, I hear my computer chime. It's an IM from Daria. She tells me she got me an interview with a Brooklyn zine in a few days. Seeing as I'm not really a photographer yet, this strikes me as odd. I write down the information anyway, and we sign off.

I keep going back to my mom's last message, telling myself maybe it was nothing. But still, I have to know.

Where could I have left the phone? Is some stranger using it to call Germany?

When I finally get to sleep, I dream that I am swimming, at camp. The lake goes on and on and is extra-thick and deep blue. My mother is on a small rock in the distance. As I get closer, she gets smaller. The water gets heavier, and it's all I can do to keep my head above it.

CHAPTER 25

A FINE IMITATION

The search for my mother's phone proves entirely un-successful, and I arrive home sweaty and tired. My father's not in his office, and the house is eerily quiet. Outside my parents' bedroom, I can hear a muffled woman's voice. Elise is sitting on the edge of the bed, talking on the phone. I decide to just walk in, and she tells the person she'll call them back.

"Hi, Elise, do you know where my father is?"

"Hey there," she says while fiddling with her beaded necklace, "he's actually on a plane. He had to go to L.A. a few days early to prep for the premiere. He felt terrible that he couldn't tell you himself, but he said he'd call the minute he arrived."

I feel the need to throw something, to yell, to shake her, but I remind myself it's not really her fault. Still, seeing her sitting on my mother's bed, wearing that hideous brown blouse and staring at me with a stupid sympathy smile makes it really hard.

"You okay?"

I am suddenly void of defenses.

"No," I say, softer than I mean. "It's just, I knew he had to go, but he's never left without saying goodbye."

"Come, sit. I know it may seem weird that I'm here and your father's not, but there is crazy construction going on in my building and he told me to stay."

"It's cool, but can we not be in this room?"

"Sure, I was actually just leaving anyway. I'll grab my things and meet you in the kitchen—cool enough?"

"Okay."

I fix myself a sandwich with turkey and mayonnaise, but after a few bites I realize I'm not really hungry. When Elise walks into the kitchen she has an air of ease that tells me she knows something I don't.

"Did you know my mother?" I ask as she pours herself some juice.

"Not really," she says softly. "Just met her briefly once or twice. Do you miss her?"

"Duh."

"I know, silly question."

"Has my father ever talked to you about her death?"

"No," she says, but I know she's lying, 'cause I saw this special on TV where they showed the common signs of fibbing. She scratched her head while she answered and didn't look me in the eye. Sometimes adults are like holograms.

"Well, he seems to be holding something back from me and it's really annoying."

She looks at me, unable to come up with a quick reply, so I change the subject. "So, when is Dad coming back?"

Elise finishes her juice and starts to put on her shawl. Do people wear shawls anymore? Strangely enough, she pulls it off pretty well.

"Not exactly sure. He asked me to pick up Tile from—"

"I got it. I'll get him."

She stops, like she's about to protest, but then hops over to me and gives me an awkward kiss on the cheek.

"Okay, bye then."

Before she leaves, she turns around and I think, *Oh no, here it comes.*

"Hey, if you ever want to talk, I'm here."

Barf.

"Sure, thanks."

She closes the door. It's not that I don't like her; I just don't *want* to like her.

CHAPTER 26

LARGER THAN LIFE

A few minutes later I leave to get Tile. On our way back home, we talk about Dad leaving early, and since we have the house to ourselves, he wants to order pizza for dinner.

"Dad gave me a credit card," he says. "Carte blanche."

"Oh yeah, what are you going to buy?"

"A vintage Vespa."

"Cool."

We round the corner to our street, and at the sight of Oliver's stoop my heart sinks. How could he just forget about me? Was it something I did? Tile, as if reading my thoughts, says, "Don't worry, Moon, he'll come around."

I smile and we turn to head up our own stoop. After we both work on our homework a little, we decide to finish the film we started in remembrance of our mother. I arrange the best clips on the video-editing software, and add a sound track of the Shins. It works nicely and Tile is impressed. She looks so beautiful, and I realize it's something I couldn't really see before, when she was simply my mother. Now that she's gone, her beauty is clearer, like opening the blinds to a perfect summer day. When she was living, her spirit was contained, and now she seems larger than life. Is that why some artists don't get recognized until they're dead? I ponder this as Tile runs downstairs to get the pizza.

I save the movie and post it on YouTube. I call it *A Day in the Life of Marion Clover*. In the box, I type, "Edited by Luna, Shot by Tile." After it uploads, I go downstairs, where Tile is already halfway through a slice. I grab a piece, wrap it in tinfoil, and tell Tile that I'll be right back.

I cross the street and ring Oliver's doorbell. The housekeeper, Denise, comes to the door, again glassy-eyed and smiling. She has the little boy on her hip, so obviously Oliver's mother is not home. Before I can even ask, Denise tells me that Oliver is upstate at a rehearsal. Suddenly I feel stupid holding the warm slice of pizza, but then I realize that Felipe would probably love it.

"Would he want . . . ?"

The boy grabs it before I can even finish the sentence and smiles. Denise notices my defeat and says, "Hold on, sweetie." She leaves and comes back with a flyer for Oliver's recital.

"Thanks," I say, not sure if I'll have the will to go without being invited by Oliver himself.

"I'll tell him you came by," she says. The boy, whose lips are now covered with tomato sauce, says, "Dank you pizza."

I turn to leave, and as I look down at the flyer, I see that my hand is shaking.

CHAPTER 27

MY BABIES

I immediately start developing more of the photographs I took at school. Since he looks at me with those soft, pleading eyes, I let Tile in the darkroom with me. He leans on the wall while I soak the photos in solution.

"What are these of?" he asks.

"The Rachels, this artist kid, and my teacher. Oh, and everyone's shoes from English class."

"You're friends with the Rachels again?"

"Not really. I just took it for the composition. See?"

I hold up the image. It looks vintage and modern at the same time. The girls are clearly beautiful, but not in the obvious way. It's a different kind of beauty. They are primping in various positions, not aware I was taking the shot. The light from the rectangular windows washes over them. There's something about the picture that makes you want to stare at it for longer than usual. I hope I'm right, that it's the composition.

"It looks like a painting," Tile says.

"You're right. Still life."

I motion for Tile to step onto the stool and hang the picture to dry. He smiles and then turns really serious as he fastens the clothes hangers.

Ms. Gray comes out sharp and clear. Her candid face, her eyes humble but still holding a strong gaze. Who can just look at a camera and have her soul shine through? Ms. Gray has had a really hard life. She lost her baby boy, who died when he was eight months old. It ruined her marriage and she never had another child. One time when we were talking, she spoke his name, Will, and it seemed to shatter the room and leave us in a wreckage of silence. Maybe that's what she's thinking about in the picture, Will. Her eyes are saying, *You hurt me, but I love you.* I have a slight epiphany and realize that should be the name of my show if I get one.

"I'm writing a treatment," Tile says, hanging up Ms. Gray.

"Cool. I may be doing a photography show."

"Duh," he says.

"I mean, like a real one."

"Is Oliver going to come?"

I glance at the negative of the shot of the Rachels. Something about it is deceiving, mysterious. It's the opposite of the Ms. Gray shot.

"Not sure. What's your treatment about?"

"Butterflies," he says, like that's an obvious choice.

"Butterflies that talk?"

"I haven't figured that out yet."

The shot of my classmates' feet up on the desks comes out very nice. Again, I think the composition works.

I hang up the last shot of the stoner kid drawing on the sidewalk. It's my favorite, but it's hard to say why. It's just the way I feel when I look at it. I wonder if the critics, if there are any, are just going to rip me to shreds. I won't use my last name so that no one can make the connection to my father. It's more about pride than anger. These are my babies.

CHAPTER 28

SELF-PORTRAIT

I put some of Tile's favorite cookies in the oven, and while he watches Animal Planet I go into my father's office and find the number for Mom's cell phone. It goes right to voice mail, but when I press Star it doesn't ask me for the password. I try again using Pound. Nope. Maybe she didn't have the option to check her voice mail from another phone? I realize that in frantically trying to retrieve the message, I forgot to even listen to my mother's voice. I call again, and halfway through decide it's a little disturbing. But truthfully, her voice was something that always soothed me, and she barely ever raised it. It was a soft, lilting tone, almost like her words covered me in a blanket.

I find the number for Dad's messenger service in his old-school Rolodex and order a pickup. Before I leave, I take one last look at his space, covered with pictures I took with my first camera. I scan them to see if any are worth including in my portfolio. In the corner is a self-portrait. I must have been holding the camera out 'cause you can see only half of my arm. I'm wearing a fluffy white sweater and my cheeks are rosy. I have one hand on my mother's pink dress, which I'm still small enough to hide under. I look really happy. I carefully peel it off the wall.

I Google my mother's name and the date of the accident, and still find only the words "a friend" regarding who was with her—nothing about Cole. Some of the articles quote her book. She would've loved that. Others call her the "anti-pinup" and an "unlikely poster girl." They all say it was a tragedy, and that she was beautiful. Some are forums where people comment. A few of the comments are really mean, saying that she slept her way to the top, that her book was trash, *blah blah blah*. A response farther down catches my eye: "She was much more than a model and a writer, she had a big heart and an open mind, two qualities you haters obviously lack." I look at the screen name that posted it and shudder: *ColeTrain*.

Oliver's window is dark, as usual. No more cello, no more silhouettes. I play our time back in my head, try to think of something I did, some catalyst that would've made him retreat. I remember the confidence he had when we first called Cole and try to use some of it to call him myself. I dial quickly and he answers on the second ring.

"Look," I find myself telling him, "I don't want to bug you, I mean, I guess I should hate you or something but I don't, I just need to know more about what happened. You said he was distraught."

"Why don't you ask him?"

"He's conveniently out of town."

"Well, I'm about to board a plane as well. And I think you should really hear it from him."

"Tell me one thing," I say, feeling my eyes start to sting a little, then blur from welling up with tears. "Did you love her?"

There is silence for a minute, and it seems as if he's choked up as well.

"Yes, I did."

"Why would she just walk into a cab?"

"She was in a hurry."

"Why?"

I can hear an announcement in the background.

"Look, I have to go. You can call me in a few hours."

"That's okay." I feel defeated, and hang up.

I watch the video I edited for Tile, and it actually soothes me. I watch it over and over, noticing the parts where the light makes my mother angelic, as if the sun's rays were special fingers that could touch her, lift her up, and pull her away.

CHAPTER 29

KINDRED SPIRITS

In the morning, I messenger Daria all the pictures, including the old self-portrait. An hour later, she IMs me, telling me she loves them. She types "omg" like ten times. Part of me is thrilled but another part is angry. It's unfair that I can't share this with my mother. When she'd have dinner parties, she'd often tell the story of how, at three years old, I rearranged and redecorated my room. And how a woman who had just written a book on feng shui said I knew what I was doing. I guess I always did have an eye for composition.

My father still hasn't called, and I can't call him 'cause it's too early in L.A. The first time we went there I remember waking up when it was dark every day. It was eerie. We had this strange nanny who wore wide-brimmed hats and smelled spicy. She told me rats lived in the palm trees. Ever since then, I've never really liked L.A. What a terrible thing to tell a child.

I realize that there's one more diary section of Mom's file I haven't read, so I head over to the studio. If I can't hear the last message, maybe there will be a clue in her last entry.

It's another nice day and there are lots of kids around. On Saturdays in my neighborhood, they all come out of the woodwork and you can hear lots of yelling, laughing, crying, and general mayhem.

When I get to my mother's studio, I imagine myself a little older, living there alone, coming home from work. Taking a bath, calling a best friend, having a glass of wine. Making dinner for Oliver. If only.

The last entry was written the night before her death:

> . . . have become such a little adult. You have a brain like Richard's, quick and clever. You have your father's creative vision . . . and like him you work from the heart outward . . . you are my

Wait a second. That's it? She just stopped there? What did she mean? *Daughter? Friend?*

The weird thing is, it feels like a goodbye. Was she going to run off with Cole to Europe? She would never do that to Tile, or me. Or would she? Did that angelic woman in the video have a dark side she never showed to the world? Do we all?

I hear my mother's landline ring. Who would be calling her a year after she died?

The caller ID says *Private Number.* I decide to just answer it. How can I not?

"Hello?"

They hang up, and for a second it all seems like some sort of game, like that movie with Michael Douglas. I wonder if more people are going to call my mother's phone, not realizing she died. I hold the receiver close to my chest. I'm not ready to let it go just yet.

CHAPTER 30

RAW VISION

I notice the clock on the stove, still accurate, and think: *Time never stops*. Girls aren't supposed to think about death, but it feels like a heavy backpack I have to carry with me everywhere I go. Especially standing right here, in my mother's former space. This cutting board, this blender, all these things that were last touched by her. I shiver and realize I'm late for a meeting Daria set up with the gallery owner.

On the street I pass a Hispanic man who smiles at me so wide I can't help but smile back. I go down the subway stairs and the train is there. Just as I'm putting on my iPod I look to my left and see the back of a kid's head with curly hair, and for a second I think it's Oliver. But I notice he doesn't have a book bag. The train starts to move and I crane my neck to see him walking toward a girl on the platform, whose face I also can't see. My view is replaced by the whizzing blackness of the subway tunnel, and I half smile, wondering if I dreamed it up. In all the years living across from him, I've never seen Oliver with a girl. He's not an obvious catch; it takes strong eyes to see his real beauty. I bet he'll be one of those boys who gets no attention in high school but has girls falling all over him in college. I look at the woman next to me, tall and mocha-skinned with a modern-style Afro. I notice she's reading my mother's book, and my heart feels like a wet towel. I try to concentrate on the Jason Mraz song playing in my ears, but my eyes are drawn like magnets to the back cover of the book. My mother's author photo, the one that *looks* serious, but she's really just being herself. I close my eyes for a moment and when I open them, the woman is gone.

Tribeca is very industrial and stark, but the streets are clean and there's a sense of calm that's rare in Manhattan. I find the building, and the lobby is filled with animal-print couches and a large sculpture that is shaped sort of like an ice cream cone. I am buzzed up and I panic a little inside the mirrored elevator. I don't even know this person, and I'm going into his apartment. Will Daria be there? I check my hair, which thankfully has been cooperating.

The elevator opens and the vast and virtually empty space is protected by only glass, with one section in the corner sporting a large orange rug and some comfortable-looking curvy chairs. I walk in timidly and hear a voice say, "Make yourself at home. Daria is having a moment, so it'll just be us."

His voice is calm and soft, so immediately my panic subsides. I sit down and thumb through the glossy magazines. Even though I know my pictures are good, I feel like an imposter. Too young, or too "green," as my dad says about actors.

A couple of minutes later, in walks a slight man with wild hair and kind eyes.

"Well, hello there, I'm Les."

"Luna, nice to meet you."

His hands are a little clammy, and his body language reminds me of Tile. Is he blushing?

I draw in a deep breath, then take the duplicate pictures out and spread them on the table. He spends a long minute with each, his expression completely neutral.

"You've been shooting long?" he asks after putting down the shot of Ms. Gray.

"Well, not professionally, if that's what you mean."

He pours us each a glass of water from a pitcher on the table, and I briefly wonder if it's drugged. Like Tile, I've read too many of my father's scripts.

"There is a rawness to your vision, which I'm not sure you're aware of."

"Well, I took the pictures," I say, a little too fast. I tell myself to calm down.

He smiles condescendingly, then his face snaps back to its neutral expression. With his green glasses and his salt-and-pepper hair running off his head in every direction, he looks like a caricature.

"Can you leave these prints with me?"

"Sure, I printed two copies, and I also have them scanned."

Then he just sits there like a satisfied dog.

"So, will you give me a show?"

He rubs his chin as if he's considering it.

"Not sure what the balance of this year will bring to my gallery. I may have a slot for you but tough to tell. These are strong, but I need to get some more eyes on them."

I'm not really sure what I'm supposed to do now. I should've gotten some more advice from Daria.

Suddenly I'm parched. I drink the water down in one gulp and then stand up.

"Okay, well, I should get going."

He walks me to the elevator and smiles when it opens, then shakes my hand.

On the subway ride home I'm not even sure what to think about the meeting, so I zone back into my iPod, which is playing Imogen's "First Train Home." Even though I'm lost in the silky electronic production of the song, my mind keeps flashing on the boy I saw. Part of me wishes that I *were* dreaming it, that maybe the girl greeting him was an optical illusion or some other love story unfurling.

Back in my room everything is quiet. I start learning my vocabulary for English. *Diffident. Inchoate. Verdant.* Oliver's window is covered up but the light is on.

Maybe it's just the housekeeper.

"Moon!" Tile yells from the hallway. "There's nothing to eat."

"Hang on, I'll come down. . . ."

My mother didn't cook much but she always had things very organized. She liked to spread everything out and just pick at things. Between school and this photography stuff and with Dad gone, I feel like I now have to be a mom, too. I look up at the glossy magazine cutout of my mother on the wall. I'm not sure what possesses me, but I take it down and put it in a drawer.

"Tile!"

He comes to my door and his face is red and blotchy.

"Order something with the card Dad gave you. Just make sure it includes vegetables."

"Are french fries a vegetable?"

I'm not in the mood for this.

"And wash your face, please."

"Yes, ma'am."

I go back on the photo blog and see that my entry has gotten over six hundred hits! I notice that Levi's online, so I IM him the link.

Moongirlnyc: Pretty cool huh?

I can hear Tile ordering in the hallway, racking up the bill, I'm sure.

Leviphoto3: nice shot
Moongirlnyc: thanks . . . I met with this guy Les Bell
Leviphoto3: ?

Leviphoto3: you're kidding right?

Moongirlnyc: no

Leviphoto3: big deal he is

When I walked into his loft I thought it was some-where special, or at least cost a truckload of money. But why was it mostly empty?

Moongirlnyc: hard to read

Leviphoto3: you need an agent immediately . . . email jj1900@gmail.com

Leviphoto3: he goes by jj, no one knows his real name

Moongirlnyc: sounds pretentious

Leviphoto3: he's a bit of a tool, but most agents are

Moongirlnyc: what do I do?

Leviphoto3: send him three jpegs (sharpened)

Leviphoto3: tell him you may have something happening with Les

Moongirlnyc: k

Leviphoto3: and you can mention me . . . jeez, you work fast

Moongirlnyc: I'm going to email him now

Leviphoto3: my point exactly

Moongirlnyc: thanks so much

Leviphoto3: maybe you can introduce me to Les if all goes smoothly?

Moongirlnyc: of course

Leviphoto3: ☺ good luck

I email JJ and he responds within five minutes from his iPhone.

Luna—
Promising. Can you be at my office 3:30 tomorrow
with prints?
JJ

Wow. Will it be that easy? At least it's an actual office
and not a colossal empty apartment. I confirm and go
back to my vocabulary, until Tile barges in with burgers
and fries in big Styrofoam containers, a ketchup packet in
his teeth. I redirect him downstairs and we eat at the
table. My mother preferred to graze in the kitchen, usually wearing a simple dress and a thin silver choker end-
ing in a leaf that rested gracefully in the crook of her
collarbone. My dad was always saying, "We should eat at
the table like a normal family," and she'd reply with something like, "Who wants to be normal?" If only I had read
between the lines.

The fries taste salty and good. Proud of himself, Tile
makes a show of presenting me with a side of broccoli.

"Your vegetables, madame."

After dinner he helps me with my vocab flash cards,
and all of a sudden it's ten o'clock.

"Thanks for your help, I've got a final tomorrow."

"Get some rest, big sis," he says, and blows me a kiss.

As I drift off to sleep, I hear the low, sweeping groan of
a cello, but I'm not sure if I'm already dreaming.

CHAPTER 31

A TIPPING POINT

I check the lost and found at school for Mom's phone: no luck. Why I had to lose it with one message left is beyond me. On my way to my English final I pray it will show up somewhere. I finish the test early and notice that the Rachels are cheating. Ms. Gray is oblivious, eating her little Tupperware container of sliced apples.

I meet Janine at lunch and fill her in on stuff.

"That is so cool! Do you think you could just blow off college and become a photographer?"

"I don't know, we'll see. My mother told me that a college degree isn't really necessary anymore, but the experience matters. Friends you make and stuff."

"I wish my mother were that cool. She basically judges everyone on what school they got into. It's such an East Coast thing. That's why I want to go to Berkeley. Will you visit me if I get in?"

I look at her slightly flushed face, with two strings of brown hair framing her cheekbones. She has always been one step ahead of me and so adult about everything, but right now she looks like a lost child.

"Of course," I say, feeling myself gaining speed on her, this school, everything.

JJ's office is in the East Village, and to get there I have to walk through what seems like a city of homeless people. I realize it's because there's some kind of soup kitchen on the block. I look into as many faces as I can, trying to peer inside their souls. They are so exposed, seemingly stripped of all pride. I wish I could take their pictures, try to capture that feeling in their eyes and their bodies, the tipping point when it all became about survival. I went into survival mode when Mom died. It was only the taste of food and the sound of music that got me through. I listened to Joshua Radin on repeat for like a month.

Before I enter the building I say another prayer, this one for Oliver.

Come back.

In the reception area I am told to sit down and wait by a skinny woman with severe bangs. I flip through *Variety* and see a little blurb on my dad's documentary. There's still a sour spot in my heart, and part of me wants to rip out the page and burn it. If he lied to me about who she was with that night, who's to say he's not lying to me about other things? As Ms. Gray says, lying is a slippery slope. Where do parents draw the line between protecting their children and letting them in on the whole truth? Before I can start to make any sense of my swirling, complicated thoughts, Miss Bangs calls me in.

JJ's office is covered with photographs and magazines, stacked everywhere like small cities. He's olive-skinned, with large eyes and thin lips. His long arms and elegant neck remind me of a proud bird. He smiles and shakes my hand.

"So, let's have a look."

I show him the shots, which I am starting to get more confident about now. He looks at them, raising a perfectly trimmed eyebrow.

"Now, you have interest from Les, I hear."

"Yes."

"Worked with him for years. An odd one, but knows his stuff." He beeps Miss Bangs on the phone and asks her for a "standard three-sheeter."

"Tell me a little about where you see yourself, say, in five years."

Something about his clear gaze relaxes me.

"Well, to be honest, the last year for me has been hard. My mother . . ."

"I know."

"Yes, well, for me I've just been trying to get through to the next year, you know? Then my father, he bought me this amazing camera, and it just felt natural, like this was the right thing. In some ways I felt so scattered and lost, like I was floating, and taking pictures is a way for me to arrange things, control something, I guess. I see composition everywhere I go."

He seems impressed.

"Well, you certainly have a rare gift. A lot of people who start out with these sort of, shall we say *edgy* prints, end up shooting editorial 'cause that's where the money is. I'd hate for you to go in that direction, as in some cases it numbs you down. What I would do for you is look for more niche gallery placements, and try to orchestrate a book deal."

"Cool."

Miss Bangs comes in with the three-sheeter.

"I tell you what, Luna. This is a standard agreement for six months, pretty straightforward. Why don't you have someone take a look at this and we'll go from there. In the meantime, I encourage you to treat the camera like a limb—always have one at your side. Almost like a writer with a notebook. When you see that composition, wherever it is, capture it."

"I can do that."

"Great. Here's my card with my cell on the back."

As I leave the offices, the homeless are now inside, aside from a few still lingering on the sidewalk. One man with red hair and a sunburned face is washing his feet with a gallon jug of water, pouring it over his callused toes. I take out my small digital camera and shoot, but then he barks at me so I scuffle away.

I email Levi a huge thank-you letter when I get home. I study math until my eyes hurt and my head throbs. Still no cello, but at the moment I'm too tired to care. Could I really be getting an agent and having a show? I realize that JJ never mentioned my father. Maybe he doesn't even know who he is! Unlikely, but I'm going with it. This Moon needs to shine on its own.

CHAPTER 32

FLY ON THE WALL

By the end of my math final my head is swimming with angles and theorems. I really have no idea how I did it, but I'm just glad it's over. The fire of that happiness is further fueled by the text I get from Daria as soon as I walk into the hallway:

I think it's a green light for your show.

I find myself jumping up and down a little. Some boys walk by giggling but I don't really care. Suddenly high school seems meaningless. I text her back:

Signing with JJ today.

Last night I had Elise look over the contract and she said it was a go. She used to work at a magazine and said it's superstandard. It was more than a little weird that she signed it as my "guardian" because Dad's out of town, but I was actually grateful.

After school I drop off the signed contract with Miss Bangs. There are no homeless people, just a couple fighting—the woman in tears, the man hot with rage. I can't help but think about the night my mother died. Was the last message from my father? Was there a scene like this on the street? I look down and hurry past, trying to avoid their drama that should be played out behind closed doors. Sometimes in New York there is no such thing as privacy. People just spill themselves out onto the streets, and it's not always attractive.

When I get home Tile is on our stoop playing a video game. For as long as I can remember, every Thursday he has gone to his friend Jasper's house. I look at him without having to ask the question.

"I'm sick of Jasper right now."

"Oh. But did his parents just leave you here?"

"No, I kinda took off."

"Tile! Uh, I have an interview for this Brooklyn zine. You're going to have to come with."

"I can stay here, I'm not going to burn the house down."

Suddenly I wish I had parents. Or at least a father who was actually around right now.

"It's cool, just come with me, but be a fly on the wall, okay?"

"I can handle that."

The magazine is called *Electric* and is housed in the back of a bakery. Tile gives the baker a big smile and gets a cupcake on the house. The place smells of cinnamon and ink, an odd combination, just like running a magazine out of a bakery. In the back we are introduced to Sal, who has greasy black hair and a silver bone through his left eyebrow.

"Did that hurt?" Tile asks.

So much for my fly-on-the-wall theory.

Sal just smiles and asks us to sit down.

"We are doing a spread on young artists, and your friend Deidre—"

"Daria."

"Daria emailed me a few shots." He pulls out a little recorder and says, "Do you mind?"

"No."

Sal asks me a bunch of dumb questions like where do I go to school, and Tile starts playing his video game. As the questions get deeper, I feel more self-conscious having Tile there, like he's this obvious sign that I'm still just a kid, with a baby brother I have to look after, that maybe I'm not this hot photographer on the rise. Tile pretends to be absorbed in his game but I can tell he's listening intently with one ear.

"What inspires you?" Sal asks.

"The way unexpected things go together. How stuff in the world can be . . . mismatched . . . but still graceful."

Tile flashes me a quick look. He knows I'm winging it.

"What was it like growing up with Jules Clover as your father?"

I don't say anything. I just stare at an old coffee cup on the table, ringed with a stain.

"We made forts out of his scripts," Tile says.

Sal apparently likes this, as his mouth slides into a wide smile. Then he notices my discomfort and says, "I take it you feel the pressure of living in his shadow?"

"Well, you are the first person to bring it up, really. I suppose I get some of my vision from him, but I don't want to be known as 'the daughter of Jules Clover.'"

"Fair enough," Sal says.

After a few more questions, Sal leads us back out through the bakery, which is now packed with people buying cupcakes. Tile recommends the vanilla to an older woman who smiles and pats his head. I don't think anyone has patted my head in a whole month, and wonder if that stage is finally over.

On the way home, Tile says, "You know, the guy just asked the dad question 'cause he had to. It's not like he can ignore it. It's news."

"What are you, a journalist now?"

"No, just a fly on the wall."

I smile and put my arm around him. I want to keep all this adult information I've been receiving away from him, but I know he's too smart. He probably already knows or at least senses what really happened with our parents. But I'm going to try my hardest to protect him. In my eyes, he's still just a small flower, and I feel like I'm becoming a strong tree. There will be storms, and he will need shelter.

CHAPTER 33

ULTERIOR MOTIVES

Tile sees the IM from over my shoulder. It's Daria asking
me how the interview went. She types that things are
happening faster than we thought with my show because
another artist dropped out.

"Do you think she has an ulterior motive?" Tile asks,
being his clairvoyant self.

"I'm not sure."

"Well, your pictures are pretty tight," he says.

I know he's saying this from an artistic point of view
and not because he's my sibling, and that makes me feel
proud. But then he adds an expression he must have
picked up from one of my dad's scripts. "They pack a wal-
lop."

The phone rings, and it's finally my father. He sounds out
of breath. I realize he's calling me from a gym, probably

one of those posh L.A. ones. I picture Jodie Foster on the next StairMaster.

"Is Tiley good?"

I can't deal with pretending everything's fine anymore.

"Yes. Listen, Dad . . ." I realize Tile is still in the room. "Why did you lie to me?"

I hear the cardio machine he is on slowly stop, then just his breathing on the line.

"Moon, I didn't lie, I simply omitted information. We went through this. It's very complicated."

I motion for Tile to leave but he refuses to. Instead, he's furiously writing down something on a pad to show me: *Get to the bottom of it.*

"Well, we're going to have to get to the bottom of it."

"Okay, okay. Listen, Elise told me about some photography show, and that you have an agent. Is this really happening?"

"Yes, if you were home you might—"

"That's great, Moon! I'm going to have Christy get on the horn."

The first time I met Christy, my dad's publicist, she secretly gave me a twenty-dollar bill. I remember not wanting to spend it, feeling I didn't deserve it somehow. I never had the chance to prove anything to her, smiling condescendingly with her blinding white teeth and her Prada bag. It was just because I was the daughter of Jules Clover. And now it's coming full circle.

"I have an agent, Dad. And nothing is finalized. We

don't need Christy. But maybe you can invite Orlando if it happens."

Orlando Bloom is the only celebrity I know as a person. Well, the only one I'm *glad* I know as a person. He worked on a film with my father a long time ago, and he actually lived in our house for a while. It was right around the time the Rachels started being really nice to me—go figure. He was so sweet and kind, and we talked a lot about silly things, not trying to be intellectual, just making each other laugh. It was the best time of my life. He has been my only crush other than Oliver. I knew he was too old for me but as Janine says, sometimes we want what is taboo, or what we can't have. It makes it more thrilling.

"Done. But you must forward me Daria's info. I have a few meetings tomorrow and Wednesday and then I fly home Thursday. I arrive too late but we'll talk the next day. I'm so sorry, I know the timing is off on this, but with the film having unexpectedly done so well at Cannes . . ."

"Right."

Tile is chomping at the bit.

"I'm so proud of you, Moon."

"Luna—that's going to be my photographer name."

There is silence, then he says softly, "I know."

CHAPTER 34

HOW COULD YOU?

The next night Elise comes over to watch Tile so Janine and I can go to Oliver's recital. It's supposed to be his practice run for Paris. In the cab on the way, we talk about my show, which is actually happening now, and I fill her in on the diary, Cole, losing the phone, and Oliver's absence. It feels good to say it all out loud.

When we arrive, Janine checks her voice mail by the side of the building. I notice there's a stage entrance and I wander over casually. The door is slightly ajar. I can see frantic-looking parents and a dilapidated table lined with bottles of water. Janine is on her cell phone and not paying attention.

When I see Oliver my breath catches. He's talking to someone whose back is to me, a girl. His hair is a little frizzy, curling in the fluorescent light. I have an urge to turn away, but instead I tilt the door open a little wider to see who he's talking to.

Honestly, I am so not prepared for what I see.

Rachel One?

I make a sound, close to a gasp, and Janine comes running over. Oliver leans down, just like he did to me, and gives Rachel a long, we-know-each-other-really-well kiss. Something crumbles inside me, the architecture of my whole body, and I can barely stand up. I feel weighted down by the ruins.

Rachel One, how perfect.

"C'mon, we're going," I tell Janine.

We walk over to the deli and then sit on a makeshift bench. It's not until we are almost finished with our big chocolate bar that Janine says, "They made a bet that they could get his attention."

"Who?"

"The Rachels."

I can almost feel the blood boiling inside me. "You're not serious. How do you know this?"

"I overheard them. I was cutting class and hiding in the bathroom."

"Why didn't you tell me?"

"I don't know. I didn't want you to buy into their crap, I guess. And I didn't think they'd even go through with it. I'm totally sorry."

"I feel like everyone is lying to me!"

She puts her hand on my shoulder and I brush it off a

little too aggressively. After a minute, she calmly explains, "They have stooped to an unimaginable low. Rachel told her little mute sidekick that whoever you were pining over, she could have within two weeks."

"What? That is psycho. I can't believe I was even friends with them. That's why she invited me over last week, to grill me about Oliver!"

"Don't worry," Janine says, taking the last bite. "Karma's a bitch."

"What did they bet?"

"Tickets to *Wicked*."

"How appropriate."

Before we get home, Janine gives me a card she made. It's a picture of a camera, with a girl holding it high above her head. It says: *Good Luck*.

For some reason, it makes me cry. She hugs me good-bye and I feel like a blubbering idiot. When I get in, Tile is asleep with his head on Elise's lap. She smiles at me and I just wave and head upstairs. I've had about enough for one evening.

For some crazy reason I sleep really well, and in the morning I head into the kitchen for some juice. Elise has spilled the sugar again, and it just might be the saddest reminder of my mother being gone. If she had spilled the sugar, she would have cleaned it up immediately. I start to wipe it up and I hear Elise shuffle up beside me.

"Oh, sorry about that. My ex-husband used to follow me around with a sponge. It's no wonder he went gay." Her face twists a little. "I knew something was wrong when he arranged the whole closet by color, including the linens."

I try to smile, but last night's revelation comes back like a jolt of poison. She must be able to see it in my face 'cause she says, "Rough night?"

I look at her and feel this strange release, as if my heavy judgments of her are vanishing. "It's going to sound petty, or obvious, but my supposed friends, the Rachels, they made a bet that one of them could steal my boyfriend, which basically happened. The Rachels I can understand, it's Oliver I cannot. He's so, I don't know, *above* them. He was the only boy I've ever . . ."

Suddenly I'm embarrassed, even though she's acting like it's no big deal that I'm opening up to her.

"If it was meant to be, he'll come around."

"Easy for you to say."

"Well, I've had my share of disappointments in the male department. In my opinion they're all a bunch of whack jobs. Your father isn't, though. He's a good soul."

The fact that she's talking about my father's soul seems odd. She barely knows him.

"A good soul who has lied to me."

She doesn't flinch at this either, just continues to sip her herbal tea.

"Well, no one's perfect."

Her answers are so generic. There must be a side of her that she's not revealing. If there's one thing I'm learning through all this, it's that we all have veneers, the part we show to the world and each other, and some of us have more layers than others. Is Elise that complex? Maybe not. Maybe what she brings to my father's life is simplicity. But my mother was not a passive woman. She would always challenge us, make us think around things as opposed to about them. She once told me that people have what is called their real voices. When you are with people you truly love, you speak with your real voice, meaning everything you say is the truth. This might be Elise's real voice.

I look out the window toward Oliver's town house.

"He hardly plays the cello anymore."

"What about last night?" she asks.

"We bailed 'cause I saw Rachel One kissing him. But what I mean is, he doesn't practice. I wonder if I freaked him out by always listening to him."

"I'm sure he loved it. He won't last long with Barbie."

"How did you know she's a Barbie type?"

"You said she was blond."

I'm starting to like her.

The doorbell rings and it's a messenger service with a package for me. I sign for it, then open it and spread the contents on the kitchen table. It's the press clipping from the zine. They printed the shot of Daria on the bench. It looks supercool.

Elise gasps.

"You're such a star. Who needs Oliver? You're getting your own show! When I was fifteen I was basically a freak. Never really talked to anyone, never mind starting a career . . ."

"How come?"

"I was just a little lost. I didn't have a dad like yours, let's put it that way. I had really strange parents."

I think about that word, *parents*, and how I will never be able to refer to it in the plural. I have only one parent. The thought makes me feel guilty for even caring about Oliver and Rachel. That's not a real problem. But it is. I can feel it inside me stirring like sour acid. Every once in a while, I suppress the urge to hit something.

I look at Elise and for a second, I see through the aging hippie to someone grounded and proud. "Maybe I can shoot you sometime."

Her lip quivers a little. "Maybe in a field."

Tile runs in and says, "Didn't mean to barge in on your little heart-to-heart, but I think there's a problem with the john."

We look at each other and start laughing, and Elise goes with him to check it out.

As I walk Tile to school, he says, "She fixed the toilet like a pro."

"Good," I say.

My mother would not have fixed the toilet. She would stencil the wall, or fill the bath with rose petals, but you'd never catch her with a wrench. Besides, she always wore dresses.

Tile turns to me at the steps to his school.

"Are you going to move away when you get famous?"

"If I do I'll pack you in my luggage."

"Deal," he says, "but it better be Louis Vuitton."

I chuckle. "Scram, kid."

I watch him take the steps three at a time and think of how fast he has grown. Maybe Mom being gone is really sinking in with him. He dealt with it so literally for a long time. She was gone. Everybody dies. She just died early. But now that he's been around Elise, he's opening up to it emotionally, and I think he's a little scared.

I am too.

CHAPTER 35

TWO-FACE

When I get to school the day before the show, I can feel that something has changed. More people look my way, smile at me, nod. The word about my show is spreading. A cute junior even holds the door for me. I've always felt celebrity-ish being the daughter of Jules Clover, but it feels so satisfying that the attention is for me, on my own accord. My photographs.

During lunch Rachel One comes up to the table where Janine and I are sitting with a couple of sophomore boys.

"Hey," she says, like the bleached-blond traitor that she is.

"Hey, Two-Face," I say. Janine giggles. Rachel acts like she doesn't hear what I say and goes on. "Can I get an invite to your thingy?"

I straighten myself up and say, "Well, my *thingy*, as you

so gracefully call it, is an event for people who appreciate art, and I'm not sure you can appreciate anything except your own hair. So why don't you trot on back to your sidekick and put on some lip gloss." She walks away in a huff and I add, "Oh, and thanks for stealing my boyfriend."

The sophomore boys look at me like I'm Wonder Woman. I feel like I could lasso out of the room and kick some serious ass.

After school Janine helps me pick out what to wear. We decide on the black dress that I got after the first message, even though I think Cole gave it to my mother. Since my father has still not returned, I don't even care if it hurts his feelings. He's got a lot of explaining to do. Besides, it's the most beautiful dress I've ever seen. Even Janine, Miss Jeans-and-a-Top, is very impressed.

"Did you invite the stoner kid from art class?" she asks.

"Yeah, why?"

"He could clean up well."

I wave a hand. "This is not about boys, this is about showing my work. Then, after school gets out, I want to visit my uncle Richard in Italy. After all this drama, I need to make sense of it all, you know?"

"Totally."

"And, this is going to sound weird, but I feel drawn there."

"Gravity, baby—it's a powerful thing."

I manage to get the dress on again, and it's still a perfect fit.

"Well," she says as she spins me around, "I must say you're not only going to be showing your work . . . you're going to be working the work as well."

I smile. I'm glad I know Janine. I cannot believe what a bad rap she got, when she has a bigger heart than half the people at school. It's stereotyping. My uncle's first boyfriend was a mechanic who only worked on big trucks. Not every gay guy wears frilly scarves and prances around. When I was younger I used to go to the park with my mother's friend Joy, a black model. People used to assume she was my nanny because she was from Trinidad. Meanwhile she was on the covers of all the rich white people's magazines. There is so much we can't know by merely grazing the surface.

We have to reach farther in.

CHAPTER 36

REFLECTIONS

An hour after Janine leaves, I find myself staring over at Oliver's steps through the kitchen window. I'm supposed to be so thrilled that my show is happening, but there's an emptiness that can only be filled by Oliver's soft smile and watery eyes. I miss him, and I don't understand what happened. With Oliver, with my parents, with all this love business that seems to cause more harm than good.

A black car pulls up and I think it's going to be him. Then I see a man in a tailored suit get out of the back, unmistakable flakes of gray in his black hair: my uncle Richard.

I run out to the stoop to make sure and there he is, standing in front of me. "How's my big girl?" I crush him too hard when I hug him and he falls back a little. Ever since I was two, he has called me Big Girl. There was a period from about eight to ten years old when I didn't like it, but now it's as charming as ever.

Uncle Richard is the one person I know who presses his pajamas. He also speaks three languages and can make a soufflé from scratch. He has a classically handsome face, with big dark eyes and a disarming smile. His pockets are always filled with mints, and he rarely cusses.

"What are you doing here?"

"I came in for a friend's wedding in Massachusetts. It will most likely be a bore. It's odd, I'm a romantic who hates weddings. But guess what? I have something for you. . . ."

"Really? Okay, come in, come in."

We chat for a while in the kitchen as he makes coffee. He starts to rearrange the kitchen a little but I divert him upstairs to show him the tribute video Tile and I made. I watch my mother and strangely enough, feel momentarily okay that she's gone. But then I realize that if she were here I would tell her about how Oliver won, then broke, my heart, and she'd probably say something hard to hear but at the same time reassuring. That's the way she was.

At the end Richard dabs at his eyes with a hand-kerchief.

"Tile shot that?"

"Yes. Edgy, huh?"

"Absolutely. Get him a script, he needs to be making features."

I want to tell Richard everything, but before I can he

hands me a box that says *Big Girl* in red marker on the top.

In the box are three things: a Polaroid camera, a burgundy scarf, and a small shell. "They were your mother's," he says, "things she had left behind at our Tuscany house. There's more, but I thought I'd start with these."

I hug him and his familiar clean mint smell makes me feel at home.

"Listen, I'm here for a few days and wanted to surprise you for your exhibition opening, but I can't stay at the loft because they're shooting a movie there and paying us a fortune to use it. So I'll be bunking here if that's okay. I spoke to your father."

"Sure," I say jokingly, "as long as you do some dishes or something."

"How about windows?"

"That works."

After he naps, Richard comes with me to the meeting with the gallery owner, Les, and Daria. My pictures are all hung in metallic frames. They look amazing. On the door, the sign is already up:

YOU HURT ME, BUT I LOVE YOU
Photographs by Luna

The gallery is perfect. Exposed brick on one side, super-white walls on the other. A view of the Williamsburg

Bridge through the fire escape. The only picture that is hung on the brick part is the self-portrait I picked from the collage in my father's office.

Les has on all black except for the green rims of his vintage glasses. We sit in the back lounge and he serves the adults white wine in small glasses, and me a bottle of fancy water. I feel like this is the last situation I could've ever imagined myself in. I try to soak in the moment for all it's worth. These important people discussing my art! JJ negotiates with a quick and sharp demeanor I didn't see in his office. There he was calm and smooth; now he is an arrow, his eyes piercing Les. He ends up changing the percentage of sales more in my favor, and getting them to black out a clause about reprints. When everything is set and we shake hands, I walk around and look at the pictures once more.

They are all reflections of who I am. An outsider peering in on the Rachels. The mystery of Daria on the bench, a faceless woman. The arm of a kid trying to draw his own magic into the world. Ms. Gray, with those unflinching eyes of the truth. A boy standing at the window, draped in shadow. And lastly, a little girl clinging to the hem of a pale pink dress.

CHAPTER 37

SPILLING THE DIRT

As we walk down Bedford, Richard takes a phone call. His calm, lilting tone is a dead giveaway he's talking to his boyfriend, Julian. I flash back to the funeral, when his long fingers on the piano mesmerized me.

As Daria tells me about the people who are going to attend tomorrow, I start to drown her out. She says something about Orlando not coming, and I basically ignore her and get right to the point.

"Can I ask you something?"

"Sure," she says, rooting around in her purse.

"Why are you doing all this for me?"

Richard tells us to hold on and walks into a deli. Daria stares at me, serious, and says, "What do you mean?"

"It's not because of my father, or . . ."

"Babe, no offense, but I couldn't care less about your

father. I just . . ." She lights a cigarette and blows it in the direction of the river, then turns back to me. "I lost my mother too, and I didn't have any, you know, female guidance, and . . ."

Now I feel bad for even doubting her.

". . . your pictures, well, they speak for themselves."

I smile and hug her. She feels skinny enough to crack. "Thanks."

Richard comes out and says, "You girls want to join me at Peter Luger's for an old-school steak? I made a reservation."

At the mention of meat, Daria's face turns into a frown. "I've got a drinks thing, but you two go, I'm sure you've got a lot of catching up to do." She ruffles my hair and says, "See you tomorrow night!"

Richard grabs my hand as we walk and says, "I had no idea you were that talented. I'm inviting *everyone* I know in New York. Which is four people."

I laugh. I know he knows more, but I'm sure the four he chooses will be characters. Those are the kinds of people Richard surrounds himself with.

The restaurant is very simple, but there's an element of class. I feel underdressed next to Richard in his linen shirt. He orders a martini and I get a Coke. It's early, and there are only a few tables occupied. We catch up about the usual stuff during our salad course, and then I decide to chip away at the veneer.

"Mom kept a diary for me. Well, she had started one."

"Really? Her book was written in diary format as well."

"Well, I hope it wasn't like this one."

"How do you mean?"

"It was weird, not like her. It had a very soft focus. I assume it had something to do with falling in love with Cole." I mention his name casually, like he was my hairstylist or something. Richard tries to hide his amazement.

"Tell me something, what was it about Cole?"

He coughs a little but doesn't respond. I know he knows about Cole, because my mother told Richard everything.

Our steak arrives, medium rare. It looks amazing, but suddenly I've lost my appetite.

"Okay, I'm just going to open the floodgates here. I found Mom's phone. There were seven messages. Through listening to them and following where they took me, I learned a lot, but I lost the phone before I could really listen to the last message. How about we make a deal? I'll tell you everything I know, and you tell me the rest. And I know you know the rest."

"I'm going to need a refill," Richard says, holding up his martini.

"And I also seem to recall you speaking with a raised voice to my father the morning after the funeral. . . ."

He finishes his drink and sort of smiles. "I'm not sure it's my place. Shouldn't you be having this conversation with your father?"

"Well, he's not around right now, and I'm sick of being lied to."

Richard neatly cuts a tiny piece of fat off his steak and moves it to the corner of his plate. "You know what? You deserve to know everything. And from the depth of your photography, and the way you've taken things upon yourself, I fear you're ready."

"I just want to know the whole truth."

"Okay, tell me what you know."

As I fill him in on everything, I slowly get my appetite back. He listens intently, looking at me with a newfound respect, even when I take breaks to eat my steak.

"The thing you need to know, Big Girl, is Marion was never one for indiscretions. They were more like soul mates. She wanted to leave, but it was killing her. I know it sounds strange, but she really never wanted to betray or hurt your father."

"When did it start?"

More people get seated around us and Richard lowers his voice a little. "They first met when she was pregnant with Tile. She wasn't showing yet, and it was basically the last shoot of her career, in Capri. I joined her there . . . Cole was the skipper on the yacht where the photo shoot took place. I hate to say it, but Cole is a good person. He never wanted to hurt your family either. As a matter of fact, he tried to cut off their friendship a few times, sensing the direction it was heading in. Years later it turned romantic, but not all the time. Being the gentleman he is, your father forgave her. She promised not to see Cole again. Then things got heavy—there was escalation in the weeks leading up to her death."

I remember the awkward moment Tile caught on video.

"The night she died, she went to dinner with Cole, and lied to your father. She called me that afternoon." He pauses and sips his drink, his eyes fighting back tears. "She told me she was going to end it with Cole once and for all."

The waiter collects what is left of our steaks. A moment later they deliver our preordered soufflé.

"Was my father there?"

Richard remains silent, a pained look on his face. I stare at our soufflé, crumbling into itself at a sad pace.

"Do you think she was really going to leave Dad?"

He sips his martini and looks out the window, then back at me. His dark eyes are kind but tinged with regret.

"I can't really answer that, Big Girl."

It's hard to get to sleep. Thoughts of my mother, and all the things she had hidden away from me, fill my head. What was it about Cole that made her turn her back on her family? I know it's crazy, but there has to be more to find out.

I get up and go to the window, expecting to see the same pulled curtain in Oliver's, but I see a figure darting away, as if wishing not to be caught. Was he looking for me? I feel that familiar blast of rage in my gut. How could he be so shallow as to fall into the clutches of Rachel One? Yes, she is pretty. Duh. But we had so much more! I felt connected to him in ways that run deeper than Birkin bags filled with designer hair products.

I stay·at the window, trying to tempt him back, but he is lost in the shadows.

CHAPTER 38

RED DOORMAT, RED PHONE

In the morning we are one big family, minus my dad. Richard and Elise are hitting it off, discussing the latest David Sedaris book. Tile's working on his treatment in his little notebook. I pour us all granola and cut up some fruit. Although I want to feel like I'm in the right place, something's missing. A small gap left by something other than my mother, but I can't put my finger on it. The last message, Oliver, my father, all out of my grasp even though I'm about to have my own photography opening. After a few moments we are all calm and quiet, thinking our own thoughts. I hear a crack of thunder in the sky outside and close my eyes for a second. *This is where it all begins.*

I overhear Elise as she calls to excuse me from school, and am quite impressed by her authoritative tone.

Richard takes Tile to school and she and I clean up. How does it become this easy? How come I am calm and at ease with this person who is not my mother? I am not sure, but after the dishes are dried and put away I feel that sinking feeling again. The place that Marion Clover used to fill. Model, writer . . . adulterer?

When Elise leaves I follow her out and sit on the stoop while she waits for a cab.

"I'm sorry I can't come tonight," she says. "I'm afraid I've got a crazy aunt to contend with. But I will make sure Tile gets there." A cab pulls over and she turns toward me and sort of bows a little. "You will be great, I'm sure of it."

As the cab leaves I stare across the street at Oliver's front door for what could be an hour. I still can't wrap my mind around why he would do such a thing. I think about leaving an invite on his doorstep, but the thought is fleeting, like our time together. Still, it was so good, so perfect, like the best bite of a sandwich, the middle part where all the flavors blend in harmony. Now all I've got is rice cakes.

I tell myself to snap out of it. This is my day. A launch at the hippest gallery in Brooklyn! How many fifteen-year-olds have that?

I take the folded-up guest list out of my pocket and my eyes scan it. Most of the celebrities are pretty random, but I recognize some names. If I could add one more, it would be Drew Barrymore. She was so nice to me when I met her that rainy afternoon. I think she'd like the photos, too. I take a deep breath, brace myself, and call Christy, my dad's publicist.

"Well, if it isn't Miss Luna, photography It-girl on the rise."

"That's me. Listen, I know it's super-last-minute, but I wondered if Drew Barrymore was still—"

"On speed dial? Yes."

"Do you think you could . . ."

"If she's in town, consider it done."

"Thanks."

"Are you going to be red-carpet ready?"

As it turns out, the red carpet is more of a red doormat. But there is a long rope, and about ten photojournalists. Once word spread that I was the daughter of Jules Clover, a buzz was created. I am not so delusional to think any of this would be happening if I *weren't* the daughter of Jules Clover, but what am I supposed to do, turn away from opportunities of a lifetime? I think not. The goal is for them to see it's more than just nepotism that got me here. Before we get out of the car, Richard squeezes my hand and says, "Teeth." I show him and he replies, "Splendid. I'm afraid you're no longer my big girl. You're a woman. Hear you roar. . . ."

The flashes start as I leave the car and are constant. I turn around and look back at the camera like Kate Winslet would've done. It's all over the top, bright lights flashing. I am elated, but nothing could be better than what I see when I finally enter the space: Tile in a tuxedo. Even though I see him every day, I can't think of what to say.

"Your dress seems to be getting a lot of attention," he says.

"What about the pictures?"

"One-of-a-kind."

I smile and tell him he looks stunning. He bows a little in response.

I walk around like I'm just another attendee, but I have a secret. In the corner of the gallery is a stairway that leads into a brick wall like a dream cut short, and I can't help but think of my mother. She would be proud of me, I know that.

I stand on the fourth step and scan the room.

Ms. Gray gasps at every picture even though she's seen them all. Her pudgy, balding date looks really bored. I love her to death, but she does need to buy some clothes from this century.

Janine is with her mother, who already seems a little tipsy.

Richard lets Tile have a sip of his punch. I secretly watch the two of them comment on my photographs, pretending to be art intellectuals or something. It's pretty cute.

Janine ditches her mom and comes up the stairs.

She points at the wall and says, "So much for a stairway to heaven."

"I need a stairway somewhere. It sounds weird, but I

just really want to get out of here, go to Italy, and try to work some stuff out in my head. I haven't asked Dad or Richard yet, but I'm going to. This show, I'm so psyched about it, but it came at such a crazy time, you know?"

"Duh. I think you're in a good space, considering. You handle stuff so easily."

"Well, I'm trying."

"Oh, look! Yummers."

The food looks really delicious: little canapés and blue cheese–stuffed mushrooms, lamb skewers. But I can't eat. Everyone congratulates me, and I feel like it's my wedding or something. I have a smile plastered to my face. After a while I go outside for some air.

I get past the smokers and go down the block out of sight.

I am staring at some steam billowing out from a grate in the street when I hear a familiar voice.

"Hey girl, I found something of yours."

It's Levi, and he's holding my mother's phone in his open palm.

My heart freezes for an instant and I say the words *Oh my god* but no sound comes out.

"The couch in our office, it eats things. I figured it was yours 'cause I went through the pictures."

"Oh, okay, thank you." I didn't even think to go through the pictures before!

"How's the show?"

"Overwhelming, but I owe you big-time. I'm not sure it would've happened without your help."

He waves his hand like it was nothing.

"You can just send me checks when you're rich."

I stare at the phone as if it magically dropped from a tree. Levi realizes I need to be alone and says, "See you inside." As he walks away, he turns around and adds, "Nice dress!"

I frantically call voice mail and sure enough, that mechanical voice I've come to know so well says, *"To listen to your messages, press one."*

It's my father, and he's slurring his words.

"I can see you, why are you still lying to me? I'm right here—"

In the background, I hear cars and what seems like screeching brakes. Then he gets cut off. I shudder and start walking down the alley. *I think I've just heard my mother die.*

The message loops over and over again in my head. There was something in his voice . . . I've never heard my dad so . . . *desperate.* Well, at least I know for sure now. He was there. He watched her die. As much as I want to kill him, a small part of me feels sorry for him. Here was a woman he always loved, who he had to fight for, who not only betrayed him, but whose death he had to witness.

I grab my dress into bunches and turn around, walking faster. I have to talk to my father and get to the bottom of this. The only problem is, my father isn't here yet.

I stop for a moment under a dim streetlight. I'm still wondering why, if my dad was in fact there when she died, he would keep it from me.

I know I must look strange, standing on Bedford in a gown by myself. I see a man across the street, looking at the numbers on the buildings, obviously confused. It takes me a minute to realize it's my father. Even though I am furious with him, his presence makes my heart leap a little. The last I heard, he was stuck in L.A. and was definitely not coming.

"Dad! I thought you . . ."

He turns, and his face scrunches when he sees the dress.

"Are you kidding me? I had to borrow the studio's plane, but I made it. One question, though. Where the heck is this place?"

I point it out. "Can't you tell from the red doormat?"

He smiles and pulls me into him. After he lets me go, I say, "Dad, I know everything. I know what happened when Mom died. I know you were there. Why didn't you tell me?"

He adjusts his tie and sighs.

"Are we really doing this now?"

"Yes."

He puts down his bag and walks in a small circle.

"I didn't want to burden you with all of it."

His eyes start to get glassy.

"Moon, you know how much I loved your mother . . .

she was, well, everything to me. But apparently I wasn't enough for her. She always said I got too lost in my work, and I didn't take the time to really appreciate her." He starts to actually cry, which is kind of contagious. "But I did, Moon. And the whole thing with Cole, I didn't want you to know because I was embarrassed. I was terrified that you would . . ."

I stop him by giving him a long, hard hug.

"Just don't lie to me, Dad. You're all I have."

"I know, Moon. I won't, I promise. You know, this last year I kept blaming myself. But more importantly, I've forgiven her. I never got to tell her that, Moon. And being with Elise . . . I don't know if I can do it. I feel so guilty all the time, I just want to move on. Thankfully I've had this film to consume me, but it's over now. . . ."

I turn him toward the entrance of the gallery and we stand there for a few minutes, looking at the red doormat, the stylish people mingling inside the windows.

"Well, for now we have to get our act together. I want you to forget about everything, have some punch, and look at your daughter's photographs."

He puts his hands on both of my cheeks, which makes me blush.

"You know, I've been a fan of your work since you were five. Have you seen the walls of my office?"

I don't have to answer. As we get closer to the entrance, I remember something I wanted to tell him. I stop him just before the door.

"I never thought I'd say this, but I like Elise. She's good people."

He gives me a skeptical look.

"Don't give up on her yet," I whisper to him as we enter the gallery doors.

The event seems to have come even more alive. Ambient music is playing; people are chatting loosely. Les walks up to me and whispers something in my ear. I can't hear him, so he says it again really loud.

"We're going to need our own lab to make all the prints that have already been ordered."

"Really?"

He looks animated. The cool artsy demeanor has vanished, and now he's a giddy schoolboy. I'm wondering how this could be, and then the answer comes, in the form of a tipsy Daria, locking her arm into his. So that was her agenda. A date with Les. Why a stunning model with legs that reach the sky would pine over a mousy gallery owner with green glasses is beyond me, but I've stopped trying to form explanations for things. Life is complicated.

Just when I think the evening couldn't possibly go any better, in walks Drew Barrymore, and the kicker is, she remembers me! She tells me she heard about my show and changed a flight so she could come.

"You're not serious."

"I am. And the shot of the kid drawing the city in chalk? I want a huge print of that for my bathroom in L.A."

The fact that she wants it for her bathroom is a little disconcerting, but I bet her bathroom could sleep ten, so I let it go.

"Oh my god, I'd be honored."

"And who is that woman?" She is pointing to the portrait of Ms. Gray.

"That's my English teacher."

"Wow. Old soul."

"Yes."

Her date, the Mac commercial guy, comes and sweeps her toward the punch table, and she smiles at me like we're best friends. But it's not a Rachel smile, it's a smile that says, *We are made of the same thing.* I almost want to scream.

Richard takes my arm and starts dancing with me, and several people take our picture. Tile is slumped in a chair in the corner, asleep. My dad readjusts his position and kisses him on the forehead.

When everyone is gone and I've almost hit a wall, I walk up to the self-portrait and try to find something in my eyes that I can carry with me. Innocence? I look at my small hands gripping my mother's dress. I want to believe that even though the world's edges have become harder, I may be able to find a warm, soft place in it.

CHAPTER 39

READY FOR MY CLOSE-UP

The next morning I wake to the sound of a cello. Not only is he playing with the window open, it's our song. I refuse to let myself be seduced by it, thinking once again of Rachel One and her stupid bet. The fact that Oliver fell into her trap has made me lose all respect for him, and that's the saddest part. I honestly thought he was better than all that. Even though I'm learning that loving someone is also being able to forgive them, I'm not sure I'm ready yet with Oliver. Or if I'll ever be.

"Fifteen!" I hear him call when he's finished. I wrap my robe around myself and step to the window, not even caring that I probably have a really bad case of bedhead.

"I can explain!"

For a second I think Tile is feeding him lines from a script, but I see that he's really upset. I simply shake my head and close the blinds. I notice my clock reads 10:15. I am being photographed for the *New York Times* in four hours. I hate to say it, but now is when I really need someone like Rachel One. Instead, I settle for Tile. He helps me pick out my outfit (simple red dress with a thin pearly trim) and holds my hair up while I apply a little mascara.

"You know what, Tile? They probably have people who will primp me."

He looks skeptical. "They're not shooting you for the fashion pages. It's an exposé."

It's clear he has no idea what *exposé* means but I go along with it.

"Hey," he says while helping me into my left boot, "you did really well last night. I think you've got a future in this stuff."

For some reason, hearing this from Tile is more meaningful than hearing it from any celebrity in the world. .

Later that day after my history final, which I know I probably got a C on, I'm shot by the *Times*. It's done in a white studio, and the photographer is bald and European. His assistants, and I'm serious, are called Hans and Franz—straight out of central casting. He makes me feel at home and we play word association. He shouts out a word and I'm supposed to answer with a word that comes to mind. It goes like this:

"Blue dress," and I say, "Mother."

"Coconut," and I say, "Cracked head."

"Yellow," and I say, "Curry," and he snaps my picture.

My self-consciousness dissipates and I exude a confidence I'm not sure I knew I had. I don't think about Rachel One and Oliver for a whole hour and a half. After, I am fed some kind of biscuit and hot chocolate while being interviewed by yet another European. She has black hair that covers most of her eyes and she asks me technical photography questions that I answer sort of like Tile would. I've read the manual but don't really know what I'm doing. She seems charmed enough. In the end, I add, "I just try to find new ways of looking at things."

I'm a celebrity, but it's the last day of school. A sophomore boy gets me an extra Jell-O at lunch and I accept flowers from a group of freshman girls. I even take one out and put it in my hair. On my way out of school, people whisper and stare.

I go to the Creperie, and even though I'm over Oliver, I feel like I'm betraying him by meeting Richard there. He loves it, though, and also orders in French. I secretly tell myself to learn another language.

He gets banana and I get ham. He talks about how much he misses Julian, but also how he can eat more while he's away from him. I keep trying to think up a way to ask him if I can come to Italy, but he beats me to it and asks *me* flat out, like it's nothing, like Italy is in Queens.

"You don't even know how much I want to do that. There's been so much going on for me, and I need to get out of the lodge."

Richard laughs quickly and says, "I think you mean, out of *Dodge*."

"I'm such a dork," I say. "But yes, the answer is yes."

"Italy it is." Richard waves the waiter down for our check and says, "We shall have to work on your father."

"Are you kidding? He owes me. I'll make him say yes."

"Well, well. A girl who knows what she wants."

On the way home I try to remember the other times I have felt this good. When Orlando lived with us, and . . . New Mexico.

"Do you remember Santa Fe?" I ask him.

"How could I not?"

My mom had our driver take me out of school one time, right in the middle of the day, and we went to the Teterboro Airport and met her on a private plane. Like the Hudson River place, she wouldn't tell me where we were going. I remember freaking out that the plane had a freezer with like six kinds of ice cream to choose from. When we got there we were quickly led into a limo. I looked outside as we drove into a canyon. The earth around us was a rich red. I was so happy to be transported to another place, and especially to be taken out of school. I was instantly someone to be jealous of. Not so much that I was taken out of school, but because I was taken out of school for a reason—one that involved private planes and ice cream.

In the morning we went to the ranch where her shoot was and there were five people fixing my mother up. Well, more like messing her down. There was a black stallion, and he was huge and fierce but had big warm eyes. After my mother got on, the horse completely lost it and started bucking wildly. My mother jumped off and ended up breaking her wrist. The horse ran into the wild, miles away from everyone, just disappeared. Even though my mother was rushed to the hospital, I kept asking about the horse. They assured me the horse would come back, but I was skeptical. Mom was immediately put in a cast. Richard was teaching in Denver at the time, and he ended up making the eight-hour drive to see us. He claimed she'd never broken a bone before.

We ended up staying at the hotel for three days, the three of us. We ordered all this weird stuff from room service just for kicks. We danced to a popular song at the time, Madonna's "Music." Richard read us some of his poetry, and my mother read us a short story, which actually turned out to be the beginning of her book. We played truth-or-dare in the hot tub, my mother holding up her cast, which was covered with a plastic bag held on by a rubber band. There were a million stars.

"Those days, that time in Santa Fe, that was probably my favorite ever."

Richard smiles his handsome smile and his soft brown eyes brighten up a little.

"It's weird because I know she broke her arm and everything, but . . ."

"Sometimes tragedy brings out the best in people," he says.

"By the way, I know he was there. But why did he feel guilty about it? I need to know. Please."

Richard looks up to the sky, all muted reds and oranges, the sun a glowing promise behind the buildings. *He has to tell me now, I can see it in his face.*

"From what Cole told me, your father followed them to the restaurant, and was drinking in a bar across the street. When they left, he confronted them. He was yelling at your mother. . . . Cole said your father was trying to pull her away from the curb, but she was disoriented. She was tipsy as well."

The last bit of color is drained from the sky and there is just a muted gray.

"She turned around to get away from him, and ran right into traffic."

"Away from him? Was he attacking her?"

"No. You know your father. He wouldn't do that. I honestly don't believe it was anyone's fault."

I start to feel my chest tighten. Why isn't there a clear explanation?

"I hate it when guidance counselors say this word, but I need closure."

"Well, you'd have to talk to Cole, as he was present. Or your father, of course."

"But he was drunk."

"Well, yes, apparently."

There's a slight wind off the park, and I try to take a deep breath to process everything. More and more, I'm thinking Italy is a good idea.

We don't speak the rest of the way home. When we get inside he hugs me and goes to the guest room. I walk by my father's office door and I can hear him on the phone. I decide to just be chill tonight and lay the whole Italy thing on him tomorrow. The only thing I want to do is watch B movies and eat popcorn, which I do pretty much all night. Before I go to bed, I look across the street at Oliver's window, which is still dark. If I could have one wish, other than my mother to come back, it would be for Oliver to be my boyfriend. To take back what he has done. And it's not like he's superhot, but he is to me. That's what matters. Is that what my mother saw in Cole? Her own kind of beauty?

As I get into bed I hear Tile's secret knock. He peeks his head in.

"What are you doing up?" I ask him.

"I think I have an anxiety disorder."

For some reason, this makes me laugh.

"Anyway," he says, "I just wanted to tell you that besides Thomas Edison and Homer Simpson, you're like, my hero."

He has a look of an old man again, for a second. Then he turns to go.

CHAPTER 40

TAKE ME AWAY

We gather around the kitchen table: my dad with his black coffee and the *Hollywood Reporter,* me with tea and the *Times,* and Tile with toast and his crumpled math homework. It's strange to think that two nights ago I was on a red carpet. I frantically search the paper for my story. When I see it, I feel a little deflated. It's more like a mention. The small picture makes me look pasty and they mention my dad in the first sentence. *Oh well, it is the* Times, *though.* I show Tile.

"You should get it laminated," he says. "Or frame it."

My father grabs it and whoops a little.

"That's my Moon River."

Richard comes in and makes a beeline for the pot of still-steaming coffee. I decide to just take the plunge.

"Dad, I think it would be best if I went to Italy with Richard for a while."

Tile stops eating his toast and Richard busies himself with the sugar. Dad plops down his *Hollywood Reporter*.

"It's something I need to do," I add.

Dad looks at Richard, who takes a quick sip and smiles. "She'll be in good hands."

"What about me?" Tile wants to know.

"You have camp," I tell him.

"So."

"So, you love camp."

"Yeah, when I was seven."

I give him a look and he stops. Dad turns to me and says, "You can go on one condition."

I start to picture myself in Italy, walking on a cliff over the sea.

"What?"

We all wait for his response.

"You take a lot of pictures."

I jump out of my chair and kiss him on the cheek.

"Can I go next year?" Tile asks.

"We'll see, Tiley."

I can't believe how fast it happens. Dad calls the airline and gets me on Richard's flight using his miles. I am so excited, I drag Richard up to my room so that he can help me pick out what to pack. I am so consumed I don't even notice that Oliver is playing. Richard is explaining to me where they live, in a small town in Tuscany where there are olive trees and a huge garden, and next door is an old lady who makes the best olive oil in Europe. I start to zone out and walk toward the window, and I realize

Oliver's playing a new song, something really pretty but a little sad.

Richard walks up behind me and says, "Hmm, he really has great tone."

When he leaves I sit down and listen a while longer. Something inside me still wants him. Is that pathetic?

I go for a long walk with my dad around the outskirts of the park and it feels good just to talk. Now that most everything is out in the open, it seems easier to digest.

"Moon, you probably won't know what this means until you have a child of your own, but I was lying to protect you. The problem is, I couldn't hide it from you forever. You are old enough to know."

The sun breaks through the trees and all the anger I felt toward him is slightly lifted, maybe because he was so nice about letting me go abroad. To be honest, I'm angrier with my mother. But what's the point of holding a grudge against someone who's not alive?

"Do you really think she was going to stop seeing him?"

"I can't say, Moon, but I do know one thing. She never wanted to hurt you."

"Well, she did. All of us."

"I guess so."

"Did you push her into the street?"

"No. But . . . the point is . . ."

"She's gone. I know."

"Yes."

I will still have to get the full details from Cole. From

the look on my father's face, I couldn't possibly pry further.

"Do you think Tile is going to be all right?"

He looks like he might cry, but then messes up my hair a little. I know I'm growing out of people patting my head, but Dad will probably do it forever, and with him I don't mind.

"I think we all just need to help each other," he says.

"Yeah."

I show him Mom's phone and he holds it carefully, as if she might jump out of it at any second.

"The pictures," I tell him, "they're almost all of you. You were her whole life."

He flips through them, smiling.

"Actually, look."

There is one shot of Tile and me. My mouth is pursed and you can see her hand holding my chin up, that wavy silver bracelet she never took off. Tile is making a face.

"Well, all but that one."

We reach the steps of our house and Tile is sitting there playing a video game. Dad goes inside and I sit down next to Tile. He wins a level and the game beeps in victory.

"I talked to your boyfriend."

"What? Oliver's not my boyfriend."

"Well, whatever. He feels bad. I think he's lovesick."

I look over at his window. The curtain is drawn.

"What did he say?"

"He said your friend Rachel was a fake."

"Wow, shocker."

"Moon, I think you should forgive and forget."

I stand up to go inside.

"We'll see about that."

"Will you call us from there?"

"Yes, Tile. They have phones in Italy."

He smiles and goes back to his game.

CHAPTER 41

O ITALIA

At the gate, Richard gives me his first-class seat and he takes the one in coach. "I'm just going to pop a pill or two and pass out anyway," he says. "You enjoy yourself."

As the plane backs off from the gate I feel a stirring in my heart. Yes, I am excited, but I've never been to Europe on my own. Richard feels more like a friend and less like a parental figure. What will life be like there? Will I fit in seamlessly? The man next to me smiles and reminds me to put on my seat belt. I strap myself in, knowing somehow that this trip will be all about the opposite. Loosening, letting go, feeling free. Still, there's the pit of my stomach saying, *Are you ready for this?*

For the rest of the flight I watch two movies, eat steak with a Diet Coke, and listen to the new Imogen Heap.

Everybody says that time heals everything.
But what of the wretched hollow?
The endless in-between?
Are we just going to wait it out?

When the plane starts to descend, I picture all the drama from New York falling off me piece by piece, like petals off a flower.

The ride to Richard's house is bumpy, or at least the part I wake up for. There are people on the side of the road selling fruit that looks bigger, stronger, and more colorful than the fruit they sell on Central Park West. Finally, we follow the long driveway to Richard's house, nestled in the nook of a small hill. The house is made of weathered brick and there's a major smell that I can't place. It's sweet, and very strong.

"He's basically planted a country of basil in the garden," Richard says while pulling our bags out of the trunk. "We're supplying all of Thailand."

I'm still very groggy, and I've yet to see Julian, who's on one of his bike tours. Richard leads me to a small room on the second floor. The walls are painted a deep red and there's a little window that looks over the pool. I sit on the bed and before Richard can even come back with my bag, I fall asleep. I wake up at four in the morning and see a pitcher of water on the table by my bed, along with two small plums. I'm famished, so I devour the plums while staring out the window at the first sign of light creeping over the hill. I've seen pictures, but now that I'm here I realize I could never imagine a place so beautiful. How did Richard and Julian do it? They just found each other, moved here, planted basil and plums and tomatoes, and bought the cutest little house in the world that happened to have a pool? I go downstairs and find my way out to the deck. I have never skinny-dipped when it's light out, but something tells me this is the time. The water is cool but not too shocking, and glides over my skin as I swim to the end and back. I see an orange towel that had been used by someone the day before, and I step out to dry myself off. The sun is now actually peeking over the hill, shining immense rays over the valley. I'm in Italy!

I go inside to the kitchen and open the refrigerator. There's so much food in it that my mouth drops open for a bit. Everything seems to be homemade, yummy leftovers in Tupperware. Before I can even choose something, a voice startles me.

"Early bird has arrived. How was the water?"

I realize my hair is dripping onto the floor and for a moment I feel like an intruder, caught in a strange house. Julian's friendly gaze immediately diminishes my fear. Instead of scrutinizing me, his eyes drape me with kindness. His body is long and lean and from what I can see, doesn't have an inch of body fat. I smile back and he tells me to sit down, hands me a mug of tea.

"This place is so amazing."

He beams proudly for a moment, then starts picking some fruit out of a giant bowl. As he expertly arranges a fruit salad, I try to picture myself living here, but it doesn't really work. I go upstairs to get dressed, and when I come back down Julian is still chopping fruit.

"I hear you're a photography sensation now."

Coming from Julian, this makes me blush. From what I know, he used to be a Gucci model, and then he toured the world as Van Morrison's piano player. During that time he developed an exercise regime that was a combination of yoga and Pilates, which he taught privately to people like Meg Ryan and Sandra Bullock in L.A. Now he runs bike tours here for people in the British aristocracy. Suddenly my Brooklyn photography show sounds like I starred in a grade-school play. I promptly turn red, smile, and put up my hands.

"I like the one that the *Times* printed. The sidewalk art? It has this animated quality, almost like you could step into it and watch it come to life."

I blush even more. He serves me a bowl of the finely chopped fruit with a dollop of yogurt, topped off with thin almond slices. It's simple, but it tastes like heaven.

"One of the great things about living here is the produce. Even the processed food is not as processed as it is in the States. I get the yogurt from a family up the road, and the oranges are from our tree."

"So you're a cook, too?"

"I dabble. I'm making some lasagna for the villagers tonight. In your honor, of course."

"The villagers?"

"That's what we call our close group of friends. They're quite the bunch."

Richard comes down the stairs in a robe with his hair ruffled and his eyes watery. Despite his disheveled appearance, he still looks totally handsome. He kisses Julian on the cheek and starts a pot of coffee. They speak a few words to each other in Italian.

"Okay," Julian says, seeing that I've finished. "Next course."

Richard stands behind me and rubs my shoulders while Julian fries an egg in olive oil, topping it with black pepper and what looks like fresh Parmesan cheese. He puts it in front of me and I take the first bite.

"So," Julian says as he cooks himself and Richard eggs, "you said things were crazy in New York. How do you mean?"

"Well, I get the feeling I'm far too young to be learning some of the things I did, and to have my heart broken, but that's the way it worked, so . . ."

The two of them sit down with their eggs on the other side of the breakfast island, and suddenly I feel like I'm at a job interview.

"I don't know, I guess you could say it was a lot to take in."

Richard turns to Julian and says, *"Nostra ragazza granda*

sta imparando che le relazioni sono complicate. All but ours, of course."

"English at the breakfast table, please," I say.

"Richard was just saying how lovely you look today," Julian says.

"Yeah, right. Anyway, even though Dad lied to me, I feel so bad for him. As far as I knew he was a mostly perfect husband."

They give each other what is supposed to be a clandestine look, Richard slightly rolling his eyes, and I wonder if they're holding something back. If there's more, I might just lose it.

After we finish, Richard heads to Rome for his weekly conference, and Julian goes on a "private" ride, taking an Australian couple on a thirty-two-mile loop through Tuscany. I spend the day relaxing by the pool with my iPod and the latest Twilight book. I doze off, swim, read, tan, doze off again, then go inside for Julian's famous tuna salad with cranberry and walnuts.

In the late afternoon I decide to take a walk along the road toward the square. When a car goes by, it kicks up dust in the afternoon light and it strikes me as romantic. I think about Richard and Julian's secret look when I mentioned my father.

You hurt me, but I love you.

I know it's strange, but I wish Oliver were here. He and Julian could jam together. We could laugh in the pool and splash each other like they do in the movies. If only.

I get to the small square, where some old men sit smoking pipes in the shade of a tree. A woman walks her baby in a stroller that looks like it was built in 1920. There's a small store, and I see what Julian was saying about the produce. It looks so colorful and fresh, like it all just fell off a tree into these cute little wooden boxes. I try to buy a peach but have only a five-dollar bill in my pocket. The shopkeeper lady is wearing some kind of bonnet that actually looks cool. Only an Italian woman can pull off a bonnet. She smiles and waves her hand, giving me the peach for free.

I sit in the square and watch the world go by: mostly little European cars, a couple of kids in what look like school uniforms, a hippie guy strumming a ukulele. On my way home, I pass a man on a pony. He looks at me like everything is totally normal, just taking his pony to the store.

When I get back to the house, I go into Richard's den and email Janine, describing the town and the house and the man with the pony. I email Daria basically the same thing, except I go easier on the exclamation marks. Then I call my dad.

"Yes, I made it safe. Richard and Julian are so nice. And everything is . . . just right." *Well, almost everything.* "How's Tile?"

"He's okay. Lucky he'll have the distraction of camp soon."

Whenever anyone says the word *camp*, my heart breaks

a little. That was where I found out Mom was gone, almost a year ago. On a dock, on a lake, the sun almost down, the water reflecting the trees, the sky a swirl of colorful clouds. A beautiful, terrible night.

"Where is he now?"

"I'm not sure, but I think he may be hanging out with your friend from across the street."

My breath cuts short.

"Oliver?"

"Bingo."

"What?"

"I think they have something in common."

I sink down to the floor, unable to fight gravity.

"What is that?" I ask.

"Missing you."

CHAPTER 42

MY NEW BEST FRIEND

I draw a bath in the claw-foot tub, the window open with a breeze coming in from the garden. I smell the herbs, mostly basil, and I start to imagine what the lasagna is going to taste like. I'm probably going to gain ten pounds being here, but I really don't care. I'll just have to swim a lot. When I was little and we'd go to the beach in Nantucket, my parents could barely get me out of the water. I would lie in the surf pretending to be a mermaid, or jump through the waves like a dolphin. And sometimes I'd float on my back and close my eyes, letting the ocean hold me up, the vast sky open above me, kind of like flying.

When I get back into the room I notice an old box on the table, the top of which says *Luna* in pencil. These must be the rest of my mother's things Richard wanted me to have. I sit down and hold the box on my lap for a long time. Before I get to open it, I hear Julian come home. I walk to the window and watch him wheel his bike into the shed by the pool. Then he peels his bike clothes off and steps into the outdoor shower. I get a glimpse of his butt, which is smooth and hard as a rock. When he's done, he dives into the pool, still naked. He starts to swim laps really fast, doing that special flip-turn thing. Unbelievable. As if a thirty-two-mile bike ride through the mountains weren't enough, why don't we swim laps afterward? I open the window and lean over, resting my elbows on the sill like a swimming coach observing my star athlete. Eventually, I get my digital camera out, the fancy one I hardly ever use, and take a shot of Julian swimming. You can't make out his butt, but one sinewy arm is extended and the water is a rich, burning blue. He almost looks like a fish.

I walk downstairs and out the front door and take a picture of the house. It looks more like a home than anything I've ever known.

I'm in the kitchen drinking water when I hear Julian come out of the pool. I don't look until a few minutes later, when I know he'll be dressed. Surely he's not going to walk back into the house naked?

I look out and he's picking basil, the towel around his waist. I snap a picture of his muscular back, the basil protruding all around him. A few minutes later he comes in and says, "Okay, girl, are you ready to be my sous-chef?"

I put the camera down and smile. "Sure. But you're going to have to put something on other than that towel."

He laughs, and for a brief instant his eyes sparkle. They're almost as green as the basil he's holding. He hops into the small bathroom off the kitchen and comes out a couple seconds later in a pair of shorts and an old T-shirt that probably used to be red but has faded to more of a salmon color. I remember my mother's good friend Ben, a fashion designer from London, who would always describe his collection with fruits and vegetables. "Lots of eggplant this season," he would say, "and limes." At first I couldn't figure out if he was a designer or a chef.

Julian plops a large bag of artichokes onto the table, then produces a pot that looks like it was made for a horse.

"Okay, we have to boil all these and then scrape out the hearts."

"Sounds painful."

He smiles. While the water boils I tell him about Oliver, and how he sort of scraped out *my* heart.

"Boys will do that," he says. "When I was in high school, I was in love with my next-door neighbor, Roddy Johnson. On the night of the prom we were going to elope, and go to the Chateau Marmont on Sunset Boulevard."

"That's where my dad stays!" Suddenly I feel like an overanxious kid. I tell myself to tone it down.

"Yes, well, what can I say? I had good taste at an early age." He gently starts to drop in the artichokes. "Anyway, he stood me up, so I went to the prom anyway, only to find him dancing with Jackie Bell. A pretty girl if you could get past the underbite. Broke my heart. I sat under a table the whole time."

"Somehow it's hard for me to picture you broken-hearted."

"Ah, that's where you're wrong, sweet thing. Everyone," he proclaims, putting the lid on the giant pot, "gets their heart broken at least once, some repeatedly. It's a fact of life."

"So, was that the only time? For you?"

"That was the one that really struck me. If I saw Roddy Johnson today, I'd probably kick him in the balls."

The phone rings and Julian expertly multitasks while zesting a lemon.

"Ciao. Eight o'clock, dear. Tuscany time, not Fiji time. Okay, ciao bella." He hangs up and moves from zesting to washing some lettuce. I've been assigned to chopping basil. "That was Isabella. She's a rock star in Canada. She's spent the last two years in Fiji and her sense of time and responsibility is, well, let's just say 'off.' Not that rock stars are ever on time, but she's learning, I suppose. She's got a husband who's her polar opposite. The man, bless his heart, has maps and codes and lists for everything he does. When he's not around, you really have to stay on top of her."

I give him my first pile of finely chopped basil.

"Nicely done! We're going to make a chef out of you yet. Now, I always say, a little wine while you cook helps bring out the love in the dish." He pours himself a half glass of red wine, and for me just a taste. There's no label on the bottle.

"It's from our neighbor's vineyard. The stuff is mind-blowing." He takes a small sip, swishes it around his mouth, then swallows with a smile. "It's all blackberry all the time. Jam in a glass."

I taste it and try to swish it around like he did but spill a little over my lip. After the artichokes are boiled, Julian takes them off the stove and puts on a CD of Italian opera. Maybe it's the dramatic and triumphant music, but for a moment I feel like a real chef. He's already cooked the noodles, so we begin the process of layering the lasagna. Ricotta, mozzarella, artichoke, tomato paste, basil, sweet Italian sausage, and so on. I'm a little light-headed and starting to get really hungry. When it's all done, Julian says, "We'll finish the salad later. Let's go upstairs and make ourselves pretty."

I put my hair up and decide to apply a little of the mascara Janine gave me before I left. "You never know," she said. I've never been one for makeup, but it does seem to highlight my eyes well. They're far apart, like my mother's. I used to think it was freaky, but people tell me it's exotic. Whatever it is, the mascara helps. I can't decide what to wear—everything I have seems too unsophisticated. After some time, I settle for a gray skirt with a simple flowing top.

Back downstairs, Julian's slicing some peaches for the dessert. He pours us each some Pellegrino, and without fail, I think of Dad. I remember when I was in sixth grade and I got really sick. My mother was away on a shoot and Dad flew home from his filming in Vancouver. At the time we had a nanny who cooked us strange food and smelled like peppermint. Tile loved her because she sang to him. When Dad came home he served me soup in bed and forced me to eat crackers. Later, I read that it cost the movie $150,000 for the delay. That's a pretty expensive stomach flu. But I was glad he thought I was worth it. I realize he has always been so perfect in my eyes, and part of me is still wondering what Richard and Julian's secret look was about.

"You, my friend, have one more job." Julian hands me four yellow tomatoes and says, "The size of a quarter."

I start to dice, curling my fingers like I saw on the Food Network. Julian secretly admires my technique.

"I saw that box of stuff Richard left for me. Did you know my mother well? Was she ever, you know, here with you?"

He stops his own chopping and his eyes settle on me.

"Standing in that very spot."

I start to feel very hot, like my skin is on fire. "I'm just gonna step outside for a minute."

I walk past the pool and see the hills beyond, dappled with the last light of day. The edges of the trees and the fences have an orange glow. I want to scream. How can I be mad at her? Right now, I am. For leaving me behind in this world, for screwing up what she had with my father—which I happen to know was something special.

For being the beautiful woman everyone always remembers, the one whose footsteps I will always walk in. I want to experience this on my own, but she is everywhere, and in everything I do.

When I come back in, Julian gets all wide-eyed.

"Darling, come here."

He leads me into the powder room and sits me on the little chair, dabs a tissue with warm water and cleans up the mascara that has run down my face. Then he sits down on the closed toilet lid and says, "I miss her too. I'd see her after a year and it would feel like yesterday. That's how you know when you really connect with someone. You can just click back on track."

I stand up and check my teeth.

"Did you know Cole?"

"Met him a few times. He has a villa a few towns away. Seemed very nice."

"That's what everyone says! I mean, it's kind of hard for me to blame him. But at the end of the day, someone has to be blamed, right? My dad was there, but he never would have been there if Cole . . . Oh my god, Julian, I'm sorry I'm going on and on and we have mangoes to marinate or whatever."

He laughs, and the sound of it makes me feel better for an instant. But when we get back into the kitchen, it's my mother's brother's house. I stand where my mother stood, probably drinking from the same glass. I start to sing the lyrics from an old eighties song: "Always something there to remind me. . . ."

Richard comes in, kisses me on the forehead, and says, "Did you get the box?"

"Yes, but I haven't opened it yet."

"No rush. We can do it together if you like."

"Okay."

He puts his briefcase down and says, "I'm off to wash."

Julian watches him go up the stairs and smiles. He pulls me into the hallway while he fixes a flower arrangement. "You know, that uncle of yours, it's been nine years and he's still, if I may quote R.E.M., 'my everything.'"

"How come I only met you a couple of times?"

"I was on tour for four years. Richard and I would always meet in London. But I came to the island once. You were about nine. Do you remember?"

I try to think back.

"Yes! You had longer hair, though, right?"

"Frightfully so. You had a friend there . . . Rachel?"

Figures he would remember her name.

"Yes."

"She kept grilling me about Richard. I finally had to come out to her."

"She has that effect on people. I'm just so happy to be away from her, that seems like years ago already."

"That's the right attitude. Moving on . . ."

"Yes. Just not quite sure where."

"To the top, babe," he says, and we clink glasses.

CHAPTER 43

THE VILLAGERS

The doorbell rings and Julian does about fifty things in twenty seconds, then takes off his apron and dashes toward the door. I see him hugging a woman with a gray bob and thin black glasses, carrying a bag that looks like it's made of straw.

"Giovanna! Don't you look precious. Come in!"

The woman looks like she was born in these hills, like she might have grown the peaches we just finished chopping. She gives me a wide smile and opens her arms.

"You must be Luna. I have not seen you in ages!"

She hugs me and her shawl smells floral, as if she's just spent the afternoon trimming roses. She could be thirty or fifty, I have no idea. She steps back to have a look at me. "You were in diapers before and now you look like a woman!" She touches my shoulder and then turns to Julian. "Have you any vino? I'm parched."

"Of course. White, or would you prefer a sidecar?"

She turns to me and stage-whispers, "I think he's trying to take advantage of me."

I feel myself blush a little and sip my own glass.

"No, I'll stick with some white, please. Tell me, Luna, how old are you now?"

"Fifteen."

"Going on thirty," Julian adds, handing Giovanna her glass of wine.

Richard comes down the stairs in a white embroidered shirt, glowing from his shower, and kisses Giovanna on both cheeks.

"Hi, beautiful."

"Oh, I thought you meant me," Julian kids, adding a fake hair-flip.

Richard rolls his eyes like he's used to it. It's funny, but the way they are acting around each other is exactly like my parents. I know Mom and Dad were in love, I just don't know when, or why, it all changed.

The doorbell rings again and this time Richard heads over to open it. A couple with a toddler comes in loaded with baby gear. The man is skinny and gangly, the woman curvy and short. The little girl has red hair and freckles. She runs right up to me and stares. I'm not quite sure what to do, so I just smile until the woman says, in a thick British accent, "Sorry, she's a bit forward. She's called Tamarind, Tam for short. And I'm Bridget." She reaches out her hand and I shake it. Tam makes a snort noise and runs outside.

"And I'm Charles," the man says. "Chopped liver, I suppose."

I smile. I already like these people and I don't even know them.

We all sit outside by the pool and eat grapes and crusty bread with the neighbor's olive oil. Isabella arrives last, a stunning woman with black hair and brown eyes, wearing a thin dress that reminds me of something my mother would have worn. Here I go again.

"I've heard so much about you. Your mother . . . she was like a summer day," she says, "warm and sweet, always lingering. She taught me a lot, actually."

What am I supposed to say? I settle for "Great," which comes out weird. Then she's whisked away by Julian, who apparently needs a private conference.

Eventually we're all seated around their huge wooden table, which used to be a door in a church. Candles line the room and the lights are dimmed. Julian serves the dinner while Richard keeps the drinks flowing. I'm seated between Giovanna and Charles, who with my help gets Julian to tell the story of how he and Richard met.

"The Raleigh Hotel in South Beach. I had a few days off from my superhetero Van Morrison tour—in case you were wondering, the song was not called 'Brown-Eyed Boy.'" Giovanna almost spits out her sip of wine. "Anyway, I thought I'd get a little diversion in South Beach, which was not the gay mecca it is now. . . ."

"Julian, let's pick a lane and keep driving," Richard says.

"Okay, there's this teeny-tiny bar, and they were serving some nut that was really spicy, so Richard comes in, all suave and debonair as usual, and orders a gin martini. He smiled at me, and I thought to myself, yes, I want to look into this face tomorrow. We start chatting, and I learn he's in town researching the biography he's writing, which I thought was *molto impressivo*. To show off, he throws up a macadamia nut and catches it in his mouth and proceeds to choke on it!"

The table starts howling. Giovanna whispers to me, "I've heard this story a zillion times—sometimes the nut is an almond."

"So he's sitting there convulsing and his whole face is purple and the thing flies out and lands, I'm not kidding you, *in my lap*."

"*Passare*," Isabella says with her long fingers waving. I glance over and notice that her other hand is on Giovanna's thigh.

"So, did you pick it up and eat it?" Charles asks.

"I said, sorry, I already have two of those!"

The table laughs again, this time including Bridget, who seems to be drinking wine at a rapid pace. Tam is in her high chair, staring wide-eyed at everyone.

"But seriously, he wouldn't stop coughing, so I suggested we go outside. Sure enough, he was better there. It was all very art deco and palm trees and even a moon." He glances at me quick enough for only us to get the reference and continues, "I told him he should be in pictures."

"How clichéd," Bridget says.

"No, it's romantic," Isabella points out.

"And he just stood there and looked at me, and something told me"—Julian gets a little choked up but holds it together—"that there would be no more searching. And here we are nine years later." He raises his glass and indicates for everyone to do the same. "To my wonderful Richard and his darling niece, Luna!"

We all clink and I make sure to look everyone in the eye. My mother told me that whenever there's a toast, you must look everyone in the eye. I always liked that, because then it means something more than just a boring ritual you do every once in a while.

Isabella and Bridget get up to help Julian serve dessert. I can tell the three of them are talking about more than how many peach slices go on each plate. The room feels a little deflated with Julian gone, like he was the warm air holding everyone's spirits up. Giovanna goes to the bathroom and Richard dangles a flower in front of Tam. Charles and I sit in silence.

All through dessert I notice Isabella constantly touching Giovanna, and Charles seems to be flirting with Julian. It's all very confusing to me, so I offer to take Tam outside for a while. Bridget says, "Please, take her for a week if you wish." Charles winces a little.

It's very dark outside but there are small yellow lights

on the edge of the garden, creating a halo around it. Tam pretends to smell one of the plants but it's only a weed. I watch her do this for a while and it's a welcome distraction. Then I hear the sliding door open and turn to find Bridget walking toward me and swaying a little.

"She's very keen on you," she says, pointing at little Tam.

"She's cute. That hair!"

"Right? It comes from Charles's mum."

"Cool. How long have you been married?"

Bridget laughs a little. "We're not. Not the marrying type, either of us."

"Oh."

I feel confused again. Bridget senses this, and puts her hand on my shoulder.

"We don't need a piece of paper to prove our love. Some people do, but we're sorted. Besides, no matter what happens, Tam will have both of our love and support. I think if we got married we'd loathe each other!"

She laughs again and I see there's a calm about her. Maybe my parents shouldn't have gotten married. Would that have taken some of the pressure off? Tam spins around really fast and falls down. She looks up at us to gauge whether she should cry or not, and decides to just wipe herself off and keep exploring the plants.

"Not sure if I ever want to get married either," I say.

Bridget finishes her wine and says, "Well, there are also different types of marriages. I mean, look at Isabella."

"Yeah," I say, pretending to know what she's talking about.

"Well, the pudding with the peaches bit is heavenly, you must go in. I'll stay with Tam."

As I come inside, Julian is setting out a plate for me, and Richard is in the kitchen making coffee. I sit with Isabella.

"It's not pudding," I say. "It's cheesecake."

"That's what we call dessert in England," Charles says, appearing out of nowhere. Isabella gets up and heads to the powder room. I eat the "pudding," which tastes amazing.

After a bit I decide to head upstairs to wash up, and see Isabella in the hallway, lightly kissing Giovanna. It's all too much for my brain to handle. I call good night from the top of the stairs and dip into my little room.

CHAPTER 44

PERSONAL ITEMS

Before I fall asleep, Richard slides into my room and gently sits on the bed.

"Everyone loved you," he says.

"Thanks, it was so much fun. I can't believe your life here."

"Well, it's not always about the glamour. Although we seem to infuse it every chance we can. Listen, about Isabella . . ."

"She's a lesbian."

He laughs. "No, actually. She has what is called an 'open relationship' with her husband. They are allowed to, well, stray, as it were."

"That's weird."

"Yes, it seems that way, but in some cases it's fairly natural. Anyway, Julian and I, we don't have an open relationship and neither did your parents."

"Maybe they should have," I say.

Richard looks at me with new eyes, as if I just said something profound, which is strange, because it was actually kind of a joke.

"Richard, when you look at me, do you see your sister or your niece?"

Again, he gives me a surprised look.

"I would have to say both," he says, his eyes collecting moisture.

"Why did she have to die?"

I know this is a stupid question. But it's one I don't think I'll ever stop asking. Richard doesn't answer. Instead he kisses my cheek, puts his hand over my forehead for a second, then walks to the foot of the bed to retrieve the box.

"They are mostly inconsequential things, but I saved them for you."

I open the box, and the first thing I see is a hairbrush that's encrusted with what looks like diamonds.

"These are fake, right?" I ask.

Richard chuckles. "You kidding? I would have sold it for a Rolls-Royce by now." He grabs it from me and runs his long, tanned fingers across it. "She got it at an airport one time. She liked shiny things. In moderation, of course."

The next thing I pull out is a white scarf, with small red flowers embroidered into the edges. Exactly something she would wear. It strikes me as unbearably sad. I put it on the table and grab the next item, a watch with Snoopy on the face.

"She loved Snoopy," Richard says. "Ever since we were kids. She had this stuffed animal of him, and the ears came off and it looked a little sinister. She kept it until the thing was just a pile of shreds."

I put the watch on and decide this will be the thing I keep forever. At the bottom, there are some letters addressed to Richard and postmarked from New York.

"Can you imagine?" Richard says. "The days before email."

I see her curvy, tall handwriting, the same as mine.

"I figure there's nothing in those letters you don't already know, and having a letter someone wrote is probably the closest you're going to get to them. This," he says, taking out a small red pillbox, "was our mother's, so I will keep it, if you don't mind."

"Sure. Is there anything else?"

"Just this."

He hands me a yellowed photograph of Tile and me sitting on a bench in Central Park. Our legs dangle in the air above the ground. Tile is smiling brightly, and I seem to be staring off into the distance at something that might be scary. The future?

I put the photograph and the watch next to my bed and say, "Well, that's about enough nostalgia for one night."

"Agreed." Richard kisses me lightly again and says *"Sogni d'oro"* before he closes the door. I know that means something like "Sweet dreams." My mother used to say it to me. At first I thought it was silly, but then I knew it was unique, that she wasn't your average mother. She was larger than life, and even now that she's gone, she is everywhere: in my wide-set eyes, in Richard's soft voice, in the Snoopy watch, the bling hairbrush. Even though I loved her more than anyone, sometimes I wish she would leave me completely alone for a day. But I get the feeling that will never happen. Death is harder on the living.

I hear voices by the pool and get up to look out the window. Charles is holding his sleeping daughter in his arms while he kisses Bridget, and I can see their reflections on the dark water. Their body language is completely in harmony, as if everything in the world has led up to this moment.

I get back in bed and simply close my eyes.

In the morning I notice one more thing at the bottom of the box among the letters. It's Cole's business card, with an Italian address. On the back is his cell phone number, handwritten, with a happy face and what looks like a sloppy heart. Sloppy indeed. I dress, slip the card into my jeans, and go downstairs. There's a note from Julian with arrows leading to blueberries and oatmeal. I pour myself some juice and end up drinking two glasses. The oatmeal is steel-cut and perfectly cooked, of course. I have the house to myself, so after breakfast I take a long bath, then read my book, then take a nap. When I wake up, I tell myself I'm over the jet lag. I put on my mother's scarf and tie it the way Isabella did. I go back downstairs and make myself a little cheese sandwich. The phone rings about ten times so I finally pick it up.

"Moon! So glad I caught you!"

"Yeah, sorry Dad, it's been kind of a whirlwind."

"You okay?"

"Yes, great. Coming here, I think, has given me that word you always use, *perspective*."

"That's a good thing."

I run my fingers through the end of the scarf.

"How are you? How's the film?"

"Great and great. Haven't seen Elise in a while, but we're supposed to be getting together this evening."

"Good." I can't believe I'm being so supportive of him and Elise. Shouldn't I be bitter?

"Listen, I sent you a FedEx with those pita chips you like, and your report card, and Tile put some stuff in for you."

"Okay, thanks."

"Well, say hi to the guys for me, okay? And please be careful. I know you're beyond your years, but you're still fifteen and in a foreign country."

"I know, I might run off with a band of gypsies."

"Listen, check in via email at least every other day, deal?"

"Deal."

"Okay, Tile wants to say hi."

"Bye, Dad."

When Tile gets on the phone, I can sense he's nervous but am not sure why. I hear a door shut and he says, "Sorry, I was waiting for Dad to leave. Listen, Oliver told me that he saw something, that he knows something about Dad."

"What?"

"Well, that's the thing, he was being really strange. He didn't really tell me, he just hinted at it."

This is getting weird.

"Well, what did he hint at?"

"Moon, just chill. You can talk to him when you get back. Have you had any pizza yet? Better than Ray's?"

"No pizza, Tile, but pretty good lasagna."

"Okay, get me soccer shirts. But nothing yellow. Gotta scram."

He hangs up and for a brief moment, I sigh and miss New York.

CHAPTER 45

BEETLEMANIA

As I clean up the kitchen, someone knocking on the glass doors startles me. When I get closer I see it's a girl my age, maybe a little older. Her hair is blond with two streaks of dark red and she has a tattoo of a star behind her ear.

"Oh my god, it's so nice to meet you," she says, barging right in and opening the fridge. "We need some young energy around here bad. This town is filled with winos and white-hairs. I'm Beatrice, but everyone calls me Beetle. Don't ask."

Before I get to open my mouth, she goes on.

"Holy crap, have you tried Julian's cheesecake?"

She gets some lemonade out of the fridge and spills a little while pouring some into a coffee mug.

"Wait a second, who are you?" Then it hits me. She

must be Isabella's daughter. I remember her saying I should meet her.

"Are you Isabella's—"

"Yes, but you'd never know it. She treats me like a friend. It's strange, really. I think it's just denial. She can't face the fact that she's old enough to have a sixteen-year-old daughter. Besides, I'm usually in Hong Kong with my father. That's where all my friends are. I'm here for a funeral—my mom's cat, if you can believe it. A funeral for a cat! Anyway, she mentioned you were here, so I thought I'd stop by."

Beatrice's confidence is infectious. I take the business card out of my jeans and show it to her. "Do you know where that is?" I ask.

"Superclose," she says, running it through her fingers. "Maybe ten kilometers."

I feel dorky that I don't know how long that is. She senses my apprehension and says, "About six miles. Why?"

"I need to talk to him."

"Well, what are we waiting for? Let's do it."

Just like that, Beatrice is out the door and hopping into one of those miniature euro cars. I scrawl a note for Richard and follow suit. I'm in Europe and anything's possible.

On the way she asks me who Cole is, and I fill her in on everything. It feels good to talk to someone completely outside my life, one who won't judge the situation or be biased.

"Okay," Beetle says, "but what if your dad had some part in it. How's that information going to help you?"

"Well, I don't know, but I just feel talking to Cole may be the missing piece. Give me some kind of closure."

"Sometimes it's better not to know, though. Are you sure you want to do this?"

"Yes."

"Well, just remember, whatever happens, it's already happened. It's hard to give and it's even harder to get, but we all need forgiveness."

"I just feel like I've come too far to turn around."

Beetle tells me about her mother and her girlfriends, and her crazy father (who is different from her mother's current boyfriend), and her grandmother who's on her fourth husband, and my jaw drops lower with each story. Basically, she makes my family look like the Cleavers.

Cole's villa is like a modern log cabin on a very remote road. Before I get out, Beetle says, "If he tries to pull anything, just scream and I'll come kick his ass."

I smile, take a deep breath, and get out of the car. I bet he's not even here, but it's worth a try. I stand outside Cole's door for a few minutes before ringing the old-fashioned bell. Just as I'm about to turn around and leave, he answers the door in sweatpants and a T-shirt. He lets me in like he's expecting me.

"Oh, well, hello," he says. "You must be visiting Richard?"

I nod and he motions for me to enter. He pours me a glass of orange juice, and I know it's strange, but he reminds me of my father—his tanned fingers and the way he sits on the edge of the counter.

"As you know, I found out a lot of stuff about everything. The thing is, I know it's not really your fault. I think it's actually no one's fault, you know? But I need to confirm a couple things. The night my mother died. Did you have sex with her in the studio before?"

"Absolutely not."

I tell him about the cuff links and he doesn't even flinch. "She let me use it for client meetings. In exchange, I paid the utilities."

"And why did you never turn them off?"

"I was waiting for your father to sell it."

"Okay, that makes sense. I just need to know one more thing. What went on at dinner that night?"

He looks out the window and for a second seems angry. Then he scratches his head and says, "To be honest, it was a sad dinner. Sad for both of us. She couldn't do it to Jules anymore. She didn't want to. Neither did I. I never wanted to do it to Jules in the first place. Our friendship was wonderful, and we filled certain holes in each other's lives. But then, a few times, it went farther than friends, as you know. But that night at the restaurant. That was our end."

"But my father thought you were being romantic again."

"Yes, he always thought that. But I will say, your mother flirted with everyone. So it really wasn't any different with regard to me. Believe it or not, I was on your father's side the whole time. He was so kind to her always, such a gentleman."

"On his side? So you show it by sleeping with his wife?"

He is silent for a while, treating it as a rhetorical question.

"Did he push her into the street?"

"Absolutely not. They were arguing, but he never touched her."

"Good."

A bulldog comes out of the pantry and scares me out of my seat. Cole laughs and says, "That's Tiny. I'm dog-sitting."

"Not so tiny."

I look outside and can see Beetle in her car, bopping her head to the radio. The thick trees outside the house stand proud in scattered formation. Tiny's heavy breaths, Cole humming, the smell of burned coffee. An end, and a beginning.

"I know she was feeling something missing with my dad. I know that she hurt him, but she wasn't a mean person. It's not fair that she died. It's not fair."

Now there are tears in his eyes.

"No, it's not," he says faintly.

I get up to leave and he holds out his arms. I let him hug me, because everyone makes mistakes, and because sometimes people just need each other, no matter how screwed up a situation is.

CHAPTER 46

BIG THINGS, SMALL PACKAGES

The FedEx package on the counter is addressed to Miss Luna Clover. I hear the patio door open, and Richard whistling. The first thing I see is a little folder with a one-sheeter inside:

THE SILVER BUTTERFLY:
An Animated Film by Tile Clover

There is a city where all the butterflies live. They all do human things like work, eat, laugh, dance, and sleep, except they are butterflies.

In all of the city there is one butterfly that is special because she is silver, and her wings are iridescent. Butterflies come from near and far to take her picture. She lives with her husband, Shoot, and their two children, Flutter and Strike.

The butterflies never go out when it rains because it's dangerous and everything in the city shuts down. One day, during a terrible thunderstorm, the silver butterfly decides to try and fly, because she thinks the rain is beautiful and not scary. She gets swept away.

Nothing is really the same without the silver butterfly. Flutter and Strike are very sad, and Shoot stops working for a long time.

Every time it rains, they look to the sky for the silver butterfly to come back, but she never does. Eventually, Shoot, Flutter, and Strike realize that slowly, their own bodies are starting to become silver. Even though the person they most loved is gone, she is right there, living in their wings.

I cannot control the tears that collect and fall from my eyes. I realize Richard is standing behind me, also welled up. I always thought that it hasn't really hit Tile yet, that he's too young, but in some ways he has surpassed me. He's right, she is a part of us, and always will be. But "in spirit" doesn't always cut it.

Richard takes the page and fastens it to the fridge with a magnet. I pull out the rest of the stuff my father sent me and notice a sealed envelope at the bottom with the word *FIFTEEN* on it in big block letters.

Oliver.

I need privacy for this one, so I sneak outside behind the shed and sit in the shade. If I'm so over him, then why are my hands shaking? I open the envelope slowly, my heart doing its own tap dance. Inside is a handwritten letter.

Dear Fifteen—

For the record, Rachel and I, well, we knew each other a long time ago. We have "history," you could say. A very brief history. I know it may be hard for you to understand given what you saw, but honestly, she doesn't really mean anything to me. I really liked hanging out with you, I think maybe more than you know. Sometime, I'd like to explain what happened. And then I'd like to take you out for a crepe. I saw your picture in the Times. This is going to sound really strange, but my picture was on the other side of the page, almost like we were touching. Right now, I wish we were.

Yours,
Oliver

I hold the letter against my chest and try to remember a time when I was as happy as I was with Oliver: Santa Fe, or when Orlando lived at our house. I can count them on one hand. I sit there for a while and breathe, then seal the letter up and head inside.

As I throw away the box, one more thing falls out.

A small flyer for a concert in Paris, with Oliver's name on it.

My eyes scan for the date. It's two days away.

CHAPTER 47

ALL ROADS LEAD TO PARIS

I try to fall asleep but a hundred questions buzz around my head like a swarm of bees: who put the flyer in the FedEx package? Tile? What can Oliver possibly say that will make me want to be with him again? What did he tell Tile about my dad? Should I go to Paris?

I decide that Julian is the person I need to ask first about Paris, because if I can go, he's the one to convince Richard to let me.

Beetle gives me a ride to the village and we stop at this huge grove of olive trees and I take some pictures of her. She is so at ease in front of the camera. When we get back in the car, I ask her what she wants to be.

"You mean when I grow up? Ha!"

"Well, yeah. When you grow further up."

She looks at me and squints a little. "I like you, Luna. You are very real. Did anyone ever tell you that?"

"No."

"Well, to tell you the truth, I just want to love and be loved, you know? Find something that interests me. Like right now I've been designing these cool belts. Anyway, I just want to find something that I enjoy doing and do it well. And I really want a copilot, someone I can walk through life with. I don't care if it's a girl, boy, or barn animal. Just someone that gets me."

"Barn animal?"

"Okay, maybe not that. But you know what I mean."

We pull into the square and I say, "Yes, I think I do. Thanks for the ride."

"It's cool, just give me copies of those pictures."

"Of course!"

I think Beetle is right. Finding someone to love and something you love to do is pretty much what it's about. It's all the other complications that get in the way that kind of scare me. Can I see myself being a photographer and having Oliver as my copilot? Yes, definitely. I just wish I could have a conversation with my mother, just one more. So I could ask her why. She had that—she had a copilot and a job she loved. Why did she jeopardize it? I guess I will never know, but I do know one thing. I have got to get my butt to Paris.

Beetle drops me off and I meet Julian and Richard at the café. Before we even get our pizza, I plant the seed.

"I think I want to see Oliver in Paris and give him one last chance. Is that lame?"

"No, it's romantic," Julian says. "But I'm not sure you can take the train by yourself."

"Yes I can. It's not like in the States, where an adult has to sign you in. Basically, a fifteen-year-old here is treated like an eighteen-year-old in America. Beetle's done it twice."

Julian gives Richard a look that says *She's on to something*.

"And besides, Daria emailed me and she's going to be there. She's my friend who set up my show. She spends a lot of time in Paris shooting for *Elle*, and her agent is there. She said I could stay with her."

I haven't even asked Daria, but I do know she'll be in Paris, and I'm sure she won't care. The more I think about it, the more I realize I have to see Oliver play.

"And I can pay for it. I made four thousand dollars at my show."

Our waiter delivers our pizzas and the conversation turns to Julian's obnoxious clients and Richard's unruly students, and for a while I'm just happy that it's not about me. It seems to have sunk in. I'm going to Paris.

The next day Richard has a lengthy conversation with Daria. I email my father and Janine, but my stories are different. In my father's I don't mention Paris. If he can "omit" information from me, then why can't I do the same with him?

On the way to the train station in Rome, Richard hands me a phone. "Now, listen. You must keep in contact with me twice a day. You'll be staying with Daria at her hotel.

When you arrive, get right into a taxi, a real one. There are gypsy cabs, guys who will offer you a ride in a regular car—absolutely, under any circumstances, forbidden."

"Got it."

"And here's the map Julian printed out for you, with the essential spots highlighted. The hotel, the concert hall, the—"

"What's this?" I point to a red mark over a bridge.

"That was your mother's favorite bridge. The Pont Neuf. I thought you might want to visit it."

We pull into the train station and I feel a drop in my stomach. This is it. I'm going to Paris by myself.

"I can't believe I'm doing this without speaking with your father. Please, just don't talk to anyone on the train, lock your cabin door, and hold on to your phone. If anything happens, call."

"Richard, I'm not seven. I'm fifteen. Everything will be fine. Just wish me luck with Oliver."

He moves the hair out of my face and says, "That's the last thing I'm worried about. But I will tell you this. In our nine years together, Julian and I have had to forgive each other a lot."

"Yeah, well, he didn't dump you for your supposed best friend."

Richard helps me out and waits with me until the train comes. Then he comes on board with me and settles me into the cabin. He checks the lock.

I point to the old lady getting into the cabin next to mine. "What if she tries to kidnap me?"

He smiles. "Stick with Granny and you'll be fine."

During the train ride I take out the letters Mom wrote to Richard. One is a card for his birthday, and one is an invitation to a runway show in Milan. Another is handwritten on gray stationery from a hotel in Spain.

Dear Big Brother,

It was so lovely to see you and Julian in Rome. You seem so happy together! I was glad you got to meet Cole, he has been a godsend to me. I didn't get to tell you, but Jules and I fought in New York, and he didn't get on the plane. He just left the airport. That's why he wasn't there. It was over that one time with Cole . . . and I think he knows but is getting on me for other things. We shoot arrows with such crooked courses sometimes. Anyway, I really want you to come in the summer. You have to see Luna, she's getting to be quite a girl, in mind as well as body. She's smart like you. And Tile is starting to talk up a storm. He's like a human radio with no Off switch. I am so tired of being on planes, but I've finally submitted the first draft of my book to that agent I told you about. Fingers crossed for me, please?

Enclosed is a picture of the clan. Love to you and Julian.

Marion

P.S. Isn't it weird that I married a Jules and you're dating a Julian? ☺

As the train rumbles through the night, I read a few more. Some make me laugh, and some are hard to understand. I fall asleep with the letters open around me and am strangely comforted.

When we arrive at the station, the old lady asks me something in French and I just smile. Where's Oliver when I need him? He could translate.

I go to the taxi line and announce to the driver the name of the concert hall, probably butchering it. He's wearing a suit and keeps looking back at me from the rearview. *Please don't let this be some weirdo.*

There's a lot of traffic, but I can see why Paris is so legendary. The architecture is so ornate . . . even the public bathrooms. The women are all sporting scarves and sunglasses, and even the meter maid is in heels. I probably tip the driver too much, but my dad always tips the New York cabbies a lot, so I follow suit. Plus, he got me here safely, despite the glances.

When I get to the box office, there's a pale, severe-looking man with too much gel in his hair and a fixed frown on his face. I ask him how much for the matinee recital. He just looks at me with no expression.

"For today?"

He shakes his head and says, "Sole out."

No. I did not come all this way to get shut out.

"Are you sure? I came all the way from New York . . . via Tuscany."

He's not impressed. In fact, he couldn't care less. I realize I'm not going to get anywhere with him. And I don't have any way of getting in touch with Oliver.

"Crap."

"*Merde,*" this kid behind me says. "The word is *merde.*"

"*Merde.* Can you help me a minute?"

The kid picks up his skateboard and stands at attention. People used to say my mom could get a man to do anything. I hope I have that gene too. I pull out Daria's French cell phone number. I show it to him.

"There seems to be way too many numbers. Can you call for me?"

He is more than willing. I hand him the phone Richard gave me, but he puts up his hand and with a gallant face, pulls out his own, which has a giant red skull on it and is held together by duct tape. Still, it miraculously reaches Daria.

"I'm at the Opéra Bastille," I say, butchering the name. "I got here and this mean guy says there's no tickets but . . ."

"Can you hold? Sorry."

I tell the kid I'm on hold. He rolls his eyes like it happens to him all the time. He starts to say something in French but then Daria comes back on.

"I am so sorry. Crazy day. There are like five people surrounding me right now. I left the key for you and . . ."

I realize there's nothing Daria can do about it.

"It's cool, I'll see you later." I hang up and we both say, in unison, *"Merde."*

Skater Boy takes his phone and then drags me back to the box office. He starts talking really fast in French to the mean guy, who looks inside a gray box and pulls out an envelope with a ticket inside it.

Skater Boy says, "Standing room. It's okay?"

"Yes!" I practically yell.

"Thirty-five euros."

I smile at the mean guy and he still gives me no expression. I pay him forty euros and then hand the change to Skater Boy, who declines.

"I hope your guy is worth it," he says, and skates off.

Me too.

CHAPTER 48

SPOTLIGHT

Daria's hotel is all shiny and gold, with elaborately framed mirrors in the lobby. If you ask me it's a little overdone, but I'm not complaining. I get the key from the front desk, and when I get inside the suite, I text Richard from the phone he gave me:

> Everything's fine. I only got molested once on the train.

He texts back a minute later.

> Ha-ha. Tell the wunderkind hello.

The shower has three heads and it frightens me when they all come on. I can't help but think about Oliver, and how I will finally see him again tonight. We are next-door neighbors, and I came to Paris to make that happen— weird. I remind myself I need to ask him what Tile was talking about regarding Dad, something that has been gnawing at me.

I put on mascara, a tiny bit of lip stuff, and my favorite jean jacket. I get there late because of the traffic. I should've taken the Métro, but Richard made me promise to only take cabs. The first soloist, a Korean piano player who looks like he's around ten, finishes when I arrive. The crowd goes insane, of course; at age ten the kid is playing Chopin better than Chopin, basically. The next two pieces are beautiful but sad, which is a theme I'm getting a lot of lately. There are only men in the standing room, and I realize they probably don't sell it to women or girls, that's why the mean guy didn't offer. Skater Boy knew I could rough it out. So glad he had my back.

When Oliver comes on, I feel like some stupid character in a romantic comedy. My breath catches and I put my hand over my open mouth. He's in a dark blue suit, and his hair is the same, which is so cool. I was hoping he'd show it off and not tone it down. He looks nervous, and before he starts, his eyes scan the crowd as if search- ing for something. His father?

He starts out a little tentative, but then completely gets lost in the piece, as does the audience. There were no pro- grams left for standing room, but as he finishes, I notice a stray one on the floor. I grab it and open it up to his bio.

I read what it says at the bottom and my breath catches again, except this time I actually gasp.

> This performance is dedicated to a girl named Fifteen.

I try to hold myself up on one of the supporting beams. Did he know I was going to be here? I am so proud of him that my anger goes away for all three songs. The crowd goes even wilder than they did with the Korean boy. I clap so hard my hands hurt a little. I don't listen to the last piece, because suddenly I need air.

I get outside and now there's a different kind of night energy, like anything is possible. I text Richard:

> He dedicated the performance to me!!

He texts back:

> As he rightly should!

The big doors burst open and the crowd starts piling out. How I'm ever going to find him is beyond me. I decide to wander around to the side of the building. Sure enough, there's what looks like a stage door. I feel like a groupie, or one of those paparazzi who wait outside the restaurant when my dad has dinner with someone famous. After what seems like an hour, Oliver comes out with a man I recognize from the picture on his stairway. His father.

"Fifteen!" He pushes his cello case into his father's arms and runs over to me. "You came!"

His father looks completely annoyed. I suddenly don't know what to say. Oliver motions for him to leave us alone for a minute.

"Thanks for the dedication," I manage to say.

He blushes, and I have to say, he's more adorable than ever.

"I miss you. And now that the show's over, I don't have *him* on my back. You don't even know. It's like someone lifted a pile of cement off me. That's why I . . . Oh man, Fifteen, I have so much I want to say to you. . . ." He looks back at his father, who seems to be sending an angry text. "When are you going back to New York?"

"In a week or so."

"We're going to London tomorrow, to look at schools," he says.

"A little early for that, huh?"

He whispers so his dad can't hear: "The only thing that matters for him is my cello and my grades. The pressure is beyond."

"Speaking of pressure, something I need to ask you. Tile said that you know something about—"

"Your dad. Yes, you know, that kid gets things out of you. It's nothing, really, but I did want to tell you and never felt it was the right time."

"Well?"

"About, I don't know, two, three years ago? I saw him kissing someone outside your house, and the only reason it stuck with me was that it was an actress, someone my mother recognized."

"He kisses actresses all the time."

"Yes, but I think it may have been more than a regular kiss. The point is, maybe your dad isn't perfect either."

I look up at the edge of the building where the paint is peeling. Imperfections. No, my dad isn't perfect, but he is the only dad I've ever wanted, and I feel a desire to stick up for him somehow.

"Why are you telling me this?" I ask.

The stage door bursts open and out comes the violin kid with an entourage. We scoot out of the way.

"Look, I said it was probably nothing, I just felt you should know, with everything that's been going on with you."

He looks tentative but sincere. Even though I'm wondering why I had to hear this through Tile first, it doesn't seem to matter. I'm standing next to Oliver in Paris. After a long, stretched moment in time, his father whistles for him.

"What, you're a dog now?"

"Basically. Okay, Fifteen, see you on CPW? I will explain everything."

"Yeah."

He swoops down real close, stops, and, noticing that his father isn't watching, gives me a soft kiss. I boil over with emotion, and my face feels so hot there's probably smoke coming out of my ears.

As I watch them walk away, Skater Boy appears out of nowhere and says, "Yes. Music Man is good looks. But what about me?"

I laugh.

"You're cute, but you try too hard. And the hair is too much."

He acts out getting an arrow stuck in his heart and says, "Ouch."

"But thanks for the help before, really. You rock."

I head toward the cab line and Skater Boy yells, "Yes, but do I roll?"

CHAPTER 49

AFTERMATH

Daria's watching TV in the suite. She jumps up when I come in, revealing her breasts, which are ridiculously perfect. Models are naked a lot, 'cause they're always changing clothes. But I think Daria is a bit of a show-off.

"How was it?"

"Great. He was great."

"And?"

I throw my bag down and grab a Sprite from the mini-bar.

"And what?"

I tell her a fast version of what went down and she says, "So, you're going to forgive him?"

"I think so. Think of all the things I will miss out on if I don't. You should see my uncle and Julian together—it sounds Hallmark, but they complete each other. And even my parents, you know? Most of their life together was filled with love. I know, I saw it. They weren't putting on a show for me. Well, for the most part. I was just too innocent to look beneath, you know? I idolized them so much I couldn't fathom doubting them."

Daria lights a cigarette and says, "You, baby, have come a long way from the scared girl who walked into Benjamin's apartment."

"Yeah, that feels like a lifetime ago."

I take off the Marc Jacobs and wonder if my mother would ever have predicted I'd be here in Paris, hanging up her dress in a model's closet.

We watch bad TV for a while, and I sleep really well. In the morning Daria tells me she has a meeting with someone about my photographs. I am thankful I now have JJ to handle it.

After breakfast, Daria spends an hour in the bathroom only to come out in low-rise jeans and a flimsy T-shirt with barely any makeup on. She looks hauntingly beautiful.

I call Richard and tell him that after going to the Pont Neuf, I'm coming back on the train. He tells me Julian will be at the other end.

Daria and I first go to the Bois de Boulogne, a park where tourists and Parisians sit around a small lake reading newspapers, smoking, and feeding the birds. All around the park are buildings that are so elaborate and magnificent they almost look like cardboard cutouts that could collapse from the simple touch of your finger. I wonder why some of the most beautiful things can be so deceiving.

Daria scrolls through my iPod and I'm surprised at how much of my music she knows. We both agree that Imogen Heap is a goddess and that Kate Nash is way better than Lily Allen. To my great relief, she also thinks Lady Gaga is overrated.

"What is the deal with the Pont Neuf?" she asks.

"It was my mother's favorite bridge," I tell her. "I'm going to drop her phone off it."

"Cela me semble raisonnable."

"I thought you were Latvian."

"By way of Paris," she says. "Come, come."

We rent these little silver bikes that are all over the city. You just swipe a credit card and grab a bike and return it to another spot where the bikes are. This strikes me as the coolest thing ever, and riding along the Seine with Daria and basking in the sun feels perfect, like everything I have done has led me to this moment.

The bridge is stunning, bigger and better than on any postcard. There's a woman sitting on the walkway begging, and she smiles at me like I'm the only person in the world. I give her ten euros and Daria makes a weird face but doesn't say anything. At the center of the bridge we lean over and stare down at the river. A few tourist boats go by, and then, like it was meant to be, I see a single white swan, stark in contrast to the black water.

"Maybe that's her, in another life," Daria says.

Normally I would think that was a stupid thing to say, but everything is different now.

"If she were an animal, I think that's what she'd be."

Daria smiles and moves a piece of hair out of her huge eyes.

"Do you know a prayer, like, in French?" I ask.

"No, but I know one in Latvian."

As I drop Mom's phone into the river, Daria says the prayer, which is more like a song. I have no idea what it means, but it sounds sweet and soft, like a melody in the distance. I cry a little and so does she, and we stay there in silence, the wind messing up our hair. The phone splashes, making ripples that start out strong but eventually disappear.

I love you, Mom. You hurt me, but I will always love you.

We ride our bikes to a café and order Cokes. I think of Oliver, how impressed I was when he ordered in French at the Creperie back in New York. Although I wish I could've had more time with him here, maybe it's for the best. I think of a word my dad loves to use, *marinate*. I have to let things marinate.

We return the bikes, and then Daria helps me pack at the hotel and shows me to the train. We make a plan to meet back in New York. She kisses my face on each side, three times total, and even that doesn't feel awkward.

I sleep for the whole train ride.

Julian meets me on the platform in the morning and takes me to a bakery that has no sign, in an alley next to a gelateria. We sit on the dusty curb and I tell him about my trip—Oliver and his overprotective dad, Skater Boy, the Latvian prayer-song, Daria and her mysterious beauty.

"Sounds like the trip was a success," he says.

"Well, the thing is, I think I love Oliver. But I know I'm too young to be in love."

"Darling, if you have a heart, you can fall in love."

"I guess, but knowing what I know now, I think I'll take it slowly."

"Baby steps," he says, twirling the little white spoon to get the last bit of yogurt out of his cup.

"Speaking of baby steps," I say, "I think I'm letting her go, finally. My mother."

"How do you mean?"

An old man walks by, carrying a bag of pastries from the bakery, and gives me a broad smile.

"I dropped her phone into the Seine, from the bridge she loved."

He looks at me a little funny.

"I'm going to keep the things Richard saved for me, and I'm eventually going to read her book, but I just want to get out from under the weight, you know?"

"Well put, and very understandable."

"It sucks she had to die. That she lied to my father, that she'll never look at me like I'm the only thing in the world. But I really just want to live. I want to do my photography and hang out with Oliver and travel more, be a good influence on Tile, and make sure my dad is being creative, 'cause he's happy when he's lost in his films."

We get up and pat the dust off our butts.

"Well, I want you to know that I'm very proud of you. Richard is too."

"Honestly, this trip has been very eye-opening. I love your friends, your house, everything. You guys are so nice to me, and most importantly, you treat me like an adult."

"Yes, well"—he smiles and puts his arm around my shoulders—"things are more lenient in Europe."

Julian and Richard go to a friend's house that night and I decompress by watching MTV Euro and eating lots of dark chocolate. Before I go to bed, I go into Richard's office and write my dad an email.

Dad—

This trip has been amazing. Richard and Julian are so nice, and so are their friends. I wasn't going to tell you this, but now that I'm back safe it's beside the point. I went to Paris to see Oliver, and to drop Mom's phone off the Pont Neuf. I saw a white swan that I'm pretty sure was her, even though I don't really believe in those things.

I'm learning that relationships are complicated, and everything isn't always black-and-white, and that living in the gray area can be okay. I think it wasn't okay for you, and that in some ways Mom broke your heart, and I know that's not fair. But in my memories of the two of you, there's a lot of laughter. I'm not sure how you can really forgive someone who is gone, but I'm trying to. I know she never wanted to break your heart. That wasn't who she was. And I know you never wanted her to turn away and run into the street that night. What I'm trying to say is, I get it. We lost one beautiful piece of our family, but it's no one's fault. It was the way things played out, and now we have to make the best of what we have, which is actually a lot. I love you, Dad.

Moon

P.S. Tell Tile I read his treatment. It was perfect.

CHAPTER 50

JE REVIENS

It's hard to say goodbye to Julian and Richard, but I tell them I hope to return. Beetle gives me her email address and one of her belts. It's not something I'd usually wear, but I wouldn't put it past me at this point. The flight to New York is a little harder in coach, but I have my iPod and thoughts of Oliver to distract me. When I finally arrive home my father takes me to dinner and asks me a million questions. Over dessert—his favorite, tiramisu— he tells me something that takes me a second to register in my brain.

"I've gotten you a meeting with Annie."

Oh my God. Annie Leibovitz? I almost spit out my chocolate cake.

"What?"

"She read your *Times* article. She called me at midnight."

"Wow."

"She's a great person to know. And basically the most legendary photographer of her generation. Any generation, really."

I remember when I was a kid, cutting out her photographs and making collages of them. Her portraits are like windows inside people.

"Duh. She's so amazing. I actually want to start doing portraits."

"Well, you'll be able to pick her brain. We'll drive out to her house in the Hamptons."

"Cool!"

As we leave the restaurant, he puts both hands on my shoulders.

"By the way, Moon, I was the one who put Oliver's flyer in the package. So it didn't surprise me that you went to Paris. I just hope Richard accompanied you."

"He did." Then I add, "To the train station."

He laughs and ruffles my hair.

"Dad?"

"Yes?"

"Thanks."

I can't ask him about the actress. Not now. Maybe Beetle was right—some things are better left unsaid. I know my father, and I'm sure it was just a regular kiss. I'll ask him about it someday, but I'm learning when to filter.

When we get home he puts on a movie that he claims he's never shown anyone. He shot it with a Super 8, on one of the first weekend trips he took with my mom. There are rays of sunshine shooting into the frame.

"Heaven's fingers," he says.

They're at a cabin near a lake, and my mother looks really young. She dances on the dock, and my father laughs offscreen. Then he pushes her in, dress and all, and she looks really afraid for a minute, but then realizes it's deep enough to ease her fall. When she surfaces, hair slick and nose dripping, she looks even more beautiful. You can hear my father sigh, as well as some birds singing. Then it cuts to total darkness except for a single candle. My mother smiles at the camera, lips stained red with wine. Then a shot of my father, half of his face, which looks wild with happiness. The last series of shots is of my mother in the car, singing along to the radio, the trees blurring by in the background.

When it's over, we sit in silence and stare at the black screen until my father says, "That was quite a weekend."

For the first time in a long while I see light in my father's eyes, as though in a flash he became himself again.

We say good night and hug extra-long. I'm happy to be in my own room again. As I close my eyes I hear the faint sound of Oliver practicing. This time I know he's playing for me.

In the morning, Oliver's on his stoop waiting for me.

"Fifteen!" he yells, and stands up.

He looks different. Could he have gotten taller in two

weeks? I realize my shoes don't really go with the dress I have on, but who's perfect?

"Hey there."

I am trying to play it cool, as he still hasn't really told me about Rachel One. As if reading my thoughts, he says, "You know, I had a huge crush on her when I was thirteen. Our parents knew each other in the Hamptons. She was so mean to me."

We head east and get sodas at the little cart. Oliver tries to pay but only has English pounds. All I have is enough for one so the guy gives us the other for free.

"And then, right before my recital she starts calling me, saying she misses me. And she must have said something to her parents, because even my father was trying to push it. But then I heard about her whole bet with her friends, and I felt so played. It was even worse than her dissing me when I was thirteen. I just got caught up in her game, but only for a couple days. She is so fake. It's over now. You are the one I always wanted to hang with. And I felt your presence, just before I played, in Paris. This is going to sound cheesy but I imagined . . . I imagined it was only me and you in the whole theater."

I think that might be the sweetest thing anyone has ever said to me. We stare at each other, and our eyes water with affection.

On our way back to his house he says, "Oxford was pretty cool, but really intimidating."

"Yeah, and performing classical solos at sold-out concert halls in Paris is such a breeze."

He smiles and motions for me to follow him inside.

We go upstairs to his room. He walks up to the window facing my house, and when he turns around, his smile seems so real, his eyes shining with truth. There are long angles of sunlight shooting over each of his shoulders. He moves out of the way and the rays blind me for a second. We both move into the shadow of the room and slowly walk toward each other.

He puts his arms out, and I let myself sink into him.

For the first time since my mother died, I don't feel the giant hands pressing around my heart. Instead, I feel weightless, as if someone has untied a knot inside me and I am slowly unfolding.

ABOUT THE AUTHOR

Stewart Lewis is the author of the novels *Rockstarlet* and *Relative Stranger*. He is a singer-songwriter and radio journalist who lives in New York City and western Massachusetts. For more information, visit stewartlewis.com.